NIGHT TO REMEMBER

She glanced down at the table and realized that his fingers were resting lightly on her arm. It was a gentle touch, but there was nothing gentle about the way he watched her. She felt herself giving way to his silent demand, felt her will to resist him caving in under the heat of his black eyes. When he stood and pulled her into his arms, Alana wondered if she'd gone crazy. But what could it hurt to give in, if only for a few minutes?

As Damian folded her to him, and she could feel the solid thud of his heart against her skin, everything that had always seemed important faded away and all that was left was the trembling awareness that only this man could make her feel.

With her fingers splayed across his back and under his shirt, his skin felt smooth and warm and so infinitely right.

LOOK FOR THESE ARABESQUE ROMANCES

Night To Remember

Niqui Stanhope

Pinnacle Books
Kensington Publishing Corp.
http://www.pinnaclebooks.com

PINNACLE BOOKS are published by

Kensington Publishing Corp.
850 Third Avenue
New York, NY 10022

First Printing: January, 1998
10 9 8 7 6 5 4 3 2 1

Printed in the United States of America

For my parents, Malcolm and Joyce, who never let me give up. My brothers, Maurice, Michael, and Myles, whose constant enthusiasm helped to keep me focused. Publisher, Leticia Peoples of Odyssey Books, whose help and inspiration cleared the barriers toward publication. Author, Layle Guisto, who read and critiqued my first manuscript. My best friends, Allison Joseph Carew, and Daniel K. Mackenzie, who were always there to talk to whenever I was feeling desperate. All my thanks. This book is for you.

One

Alana Britton handed over the fare and quietly said a prayer of thanks. For a while there, she hadn't been at all certain that they were going to make it. Ten minutes was all it had taken the cabby to travel the fourteen miles between London and Heathrow Airport. He had managed this almost-impossible feat by charging along the motorway, dodging between trucks, cars, and vehicles of every size and description. She had closed her eyes during the most dangerous moments, opening them only when she had heard him ask:

"Terminal Four, then, is it, luv?"

She peered out the window now, and her nose wrinkled unconsciously. It was a typical winter day in London. The sky was metal gray, and overcast with the threat of more rain. Just outside, scores of people struggled between their cars and the terminal doors. The winds ripped mercilessly at coats and small handbags, even occasionally turning a poorly-made umbrella inside-out.

Alana bent and scrambled around for a second. She had managed to keep her carry-on luggage trapped between her long, shapely legs, but the umbrella had rolled almost out of reach beneath the driver's chair. A swatch of wavy black hair fell across one dark, almond-shaped eye, and she brushed the tendril impatiently back into place. The action exposed a soft, beautiful face with high, sculpted cheekbones and a full mouth.

The cabby beamed at her as she straightened up. He appeared completely unmoved by the harrowing trip. "You know . . . you remind me of someone, but I can't for the life of me think who."

Alana smiled at him. She was still too shaken by the breakneck pace and the several near collisions to do more. She clambered unsteadily from the car and forced the sturdy, cream-colored umbrella open. The wind was damp and bitterly cold. It was a struggle to stand erect and keep the slanting rain out of her eyes.

"Here, let me help you with that." The cabby pulled his orange slicker hood up over his head, then picked up her case. "Where're we off to?"

"The B.W.I.A. ticket counter."

"The man trotted cheerfully along beside her. "Going to the Caribbean, then?"

"Yes. Then on to Guyana."

He nodded. "Ah . . . That little country in South America where that fellow Jim Jones killed all those poor buggers."

Alana took a little breath and waited. She knew exactly what was coming next.

"Tell me, luv . . . did you live nearby?"

Alana trotted out her usual explanation: *No, she had never lived close. Jonestown had been nothing more than a collection of shacks built in a clearing in the jungle. The closest populated area had been at least five hundred miles away.*

He seemed to have been satisfied with the explanation, for he galloped on to something else entirely. "Me and the missus have been planning to take a trip somewhere for the last twenty years. She's had her heart set on Paris."

"France would be lovely," Alana agreed. They were inside the terminal now, and a warm, happy feeling was beginning to envelop her. She was going home. After five years of hard study, she was really on her way home. Her diploma was neatly rolled and stored in a shiny leather case in her carry-on bag. In beautiful Gaelic lettering, it read: Oxford University. Doctoral Degree, Chemistry. The thick parchment-style paper made a crisp, official sound every time she opened it up to make sure it was real.

"Well, here we are," the cabby said. "Will you be able to manage, do you think?"

"I'll be fine," Alana said, and she gave the man a grand smile. She almost felt like pressing a kiss to one of his weather-beaten cheeks. But, instead, she said, "It was really kind of you to help me this far. I hope you have a very pleasant holiday season. And try not to go quite so fast on those wet roads."

The man grinned. "Leave it to me, luv." He gave her arm a little tap. "Have a safe flight."

Then, almost as an afterthought, he said, "That actress . . . Jayne Kennedy. That's who you look like. Faces . . . it takes me a while sometimes, but I never forget 'em."

Alana gave him a little wave as he walked off. She had no idea who Jayne Kennedy was, or why on earth the cabby thought she shared a resemblance with her. The only person she really looked like was her brother Harry. A little smile curved the corners of her lips at that thought. It wouldn't be long now. Bending, she picked up her suitcase and, with an unconscious sway to her hips, clipped smartly across to the counter.

Check-in was over in a matter of minutes, leaving about one hour and a half to spare before flight time. Alana took the opportunity to browse through the duty-free shops. This was one of her favorite airport activities. There were always quaint little stores and all sorts of interesting knickknacks to be had. She stopped before

the window of Lawley's to gaze at the gorgeous display
of English bone china, and hesitated a moment. If she
did go in, it would be impossible to leave without buying
something. Maybe a Wedgwood dinner set, or a Minton
tea service. The Lladro figures and David Winter cot-
tages were wonderful, too. But she couldn't. It would
be too extravagant. "Would you like to come in and
take a closer look, ma'am?" She had been standing at
the window display a little too long. One of the sales-
men, noticing her interest, had come out.

Alana smiled. "Thank you, but I was just having a
look, really."

She was saved the effort of further explanation by a
large group of tourists, all wearing thick sweatshirts with
España emblazoned on the front. They jostled their way
good-naturedly into the store. The laughter and raised
voices were a sufficient distraction for the salesman, and
Alana was able to slip away quietly.

The airport was noticeably more crowded now. People were dressed in a curious mixture of summer and
winter attire. There were those in bright floral shirts,
shorts, and sandals, and others still in thick woolen winter coats, ear muffs, and gloves. Mothers pushed strol-
lers with sleeping infants. Men and women, dressed in
elegantly tailored suits, some reading the London Business Times, others talking into cellular phones. There
was a general buzz of conversation, different languages
rising and falling, intertwining, and subsiding again.

This was only the second time that Alana had been
permitted to travel completely alone, and she reveled
in the bustling atmosphere. Each store window caught
her attention. She walked along slowly, thoroughly enjoying the antique engravings, the slinky dresses, the
sparkling jewelry. Even the fish-and-chips shop was
worth a look.

Outside The Chocolatier, she paused again. Some of

London's finest chocolates could be purchased here. There was something for every taste: crunchy coconut cremes, soft, succulent strawberry mounds wrapped in dark nugget, silky chocolate mints which melted as soon as they were popped into the mouth. The list was endless and irresistible. It took only a momentary struggle before she made up her mind. She would take a quick look around inside. Maybe buy a tiny box of clusters, something to munch on the plane.

The interior of the shop was a wonderland of brightly wrapped packages and pungent smells. Alana browsed happily for a few minutes until she found exactly what she wanted. She was in the middle of a very thoughtful investigation of a large box of candied sweets when a deep voice from somewhere behind her brought her head up and around.

"Those are my favorites too."

Alana turned, and found herself staring directly into a pair of charcoal-black eyes. "Oh, I'm terribly sorry. Am I in your way?"

The man smiled, and Alana felt a quick tide of heat rush toward her face. He was handsome. In fact, he was very handsome. His hair was low-cropped, his face clean-shaven except for a trim, well-groomed mustache. . . . Alana let her eyes wander quickly over his face. They flickered over his nose, lips, chin: noticing everything. He was almost as perfect as her brother Harry. Though Harry was, of course, only twenty-eight, and this man was probably in his mid-to-late thirties.

She was so distracted that it took her a couple of seconds to realize that he was speaking to her again.

"Were you thinking of getting that?" The man pointed to a rather large, colorfully wrapped assortment of chocolate truffles.

"Well, I was actually thinking of the smaller package," Alana almost stammered. She usually did not indulge her sweet tooth. What a terrible moment to be caught greedily eyeing the largest box of chocolates on the shelf. A smile played around the man's mouth, and for a moment, Alana dreaded what he was going to say next. She found herself wishing that he not introduce himself. She didn't want to know anything at all about him. What was the point, after all? Besides, no-name strangers were much easier to forget than people you knew something, anything, about. But she didn't have to worry, for all he said was: "Why don't I get this one for you, a little snack for your trip?" He picked up one of the larger boxes to give it a quick inspection.

Alana's cheeks were genuinely flushed now. Introducing himself was probably the last thing on his mind. He was more intent on buying chocolates than anything else.

"Oh, no . . . really . . . I couldn't let you . . . I mean, it's awfully nice of you, but . . ." She looked wildly at her watch and mentally groped for a way to extricate herself. What in God's name was the matter with her? She had met handsome men before, and they had never affected her this way. True, she didn't have a long list of conquests behind her. But to behave like a complete half-wit, just because he had an acceptable face, a pair of indigo-black eyes, and firm, well-shaped lips that seemed just the right size for most things, was ridiculous. She had to get a hold of herself. Maybe it was the tiny shop . . . some new form of claustrophobia. She had to get out, away from the rows and rows of chocolate boxes . . . and him. Somewhere where she could breathe again, normally.

"It's . . . it's almost time for my flight. Would you excuse me?" In her desperation to make a speedy retreat from the shop, she drove a pointed heel into the soft leather of the man's right shoe. She heard him grunt as the tip ground against his instep. They both teetered for a few seconds before he regained his balance and steadied her also. Several minutes more were spent in apology, during which time Alana even considered offering to massage the offending spot.

"I can't tell you how awfully sorry I am," she said again.

"No real harm done."

The smile had vanished from the man's face, and Alana was uncertain whether this was due to the strain that came from concealing such an obviously painful injury, or to the fact that he had now probably taken a very active dislike to her. She hurried out of the shop, and hid in a bookstore near the other end of the terminal building until she heard boarding instructions for her flight. By then, she had regrouped sufficiently. She was, once again, her rational, even-tempered self. The claustrophobia, or whatever madness had taken hold of her, was completely gone. She had bought a "how-to" book on instructional chemistry, and was in a happy frame of mind when she joined the line at the gate.

Once on board the aircraft, she removed her cream camel-hair jacket, folded it with quick hands, and placed it on the seat beside her. She wore a white wool dress cut along simple but elegant lines and a slim gold watch. Her mane of wavy black hair was pulled back to reveal the high, sculptured bones of her face, and was secured at the nape of her neck with a thick tortoiseshell clasp. Many heads turned as she walked down to hang her jacket. She was completely unaware of what a strikingly beautiful woman she was, and was always surprised and embarrassed if anyone brought this to her attention.

While she was up, she decided to select a scientific journal from the library. It was going to be a long flight, and nothing would eat up the time better than a good read. She made her selection in a leisurely manner, finally settling on a current copy of *Science*. Once she was back in her seat and safely belted in, she pulled up the window shade and stared out at the wet tarmac. The day hadn't improved. It was still gray and ugly. The kind that was best spent indoors. For a minute, she let her mind wander to the man she had injured in the duty-free shop. She wondered if he had managed to walk out from the store without limping too badly. What a thing to happen.

Her eyes followed the busy activities of the ground crew as they loaded luggage and fueled the aircraft. A snatch of a Broadway tune popped into her head, and she hummed it softly as she turned away from the window and prepared to read her journal. She flipped the first few pages without really seeing the articles. It would be good to see Harry again. It had been more than two years since she had seen her brother. A fond smile curved her lips. Harry was two years her senior, but they had always been as close as twins.

"Dr. Britton, would you bring your seat upright?" The flight attendant smiled down at her.

"Oh, are we ready to go?" Alana asked.

"Yes." The flight attendant nodded. "As soon as we're airborne, you'll be able to really stretch out. There'll not be anyone seated beside you this trip."

"Lovely," Alana said, and she settled back comfortably in the soft leather chair.

Within a few minutes, they were on take-off. The runway became a blur as the plane picked up speed. She closed her eyes at the sight of the tarmac whizzing by. She was usually quite good about flying once the plane was nicely in the air, but this was the part that made her dizzy. She clung to the arms of her chair, and didn't open her eyes again until after they had come out of the steep climb.

Just beside her, a kind voice was saying, "It often helps if you think about something else entirely."

Alana's eyes sprang open, and her lips parted in shock. "You."

It was the man from the chocolate shop. Surely she hadn't walked past him as she'd boarded the plane.

He answered the dumb question on her face without giving her the opportunity to ask it. "I was one of the last passengers on, and you were looking out the window. May I sit?" He was in the chair, again before she could reply. He flipped down the tray table, placed a large package there, then extended his hand. "Damian Collins."

Alana took his hand because there was little else she could do, and mumbled her name. So much for not wanting to know anything about him. Her hand was warmly engulfed for a quick second, then released. He was smiling at her again, and Alana forced herself to say something articulate.

"Has your foot recovered?" It was quite a stupid question, and she realized this the second the words were out. Why bring up the embarrassment of an hour before?

"You hardly did any damage at all. You probably weigh next to nothing."

His eyes ran slowly over the fine lines of her face, and she felt a surge of embarrassment, and something more, as they lingered on her lips, then drifted lower. He was quite bold, she realized. And it probably had a lot to do with the fact that most red-blooded women would find him completely irresistible. She had to let him know quickly that she was not one of them. She was a serious girl, after all, certainly not the type to have minor flirtations with strange men on planes. She would have to rebuff his advances carefully. It had been her experience that very handsome men, with more than their fair share of animal magnetism, very rarely took rejection well. She was almost certain that this one would not, and she did want the flight to be a pleasant one.

"Are you going to Trinidad and Tobago, or connecting to somewhere else?" She had purposely ignored his previous comment about her physique.

"Trinidad and Tobago," he nodded. "I'll be spending a week or so there. It'll be my second time in that part of the Caribbean. Never done much sight-seeing, though. Maybe, if you're not too busy, you might show me around?"

There was a persuasive smile beginning to curve the corners of his lips, and Alana found herself responding to it, despite her earlier admonitions to herself about flirtatious behavior.

She smiled, too, and it softened the impact of her words. "I'm not stopping in Trinidad, I'm afraid. I'll be going on to Guyana."

"So, you're Guyanese then?" He crossed his legs, and adjusted his tie.

He didn't seem terribly put out by the news that she wouldn't be showing him around, Alana noted. Not that she cared one way or the other. It was just that she was a little surprised that he hadn't even tried to persuade her.

"Yes, born and bred." She opened the journal on her lap with a crisp flip of her wrist. One woman was probably just as good as any other to him anyway. She hoped he would take the hint and not try to talk to her any further. If she absorbed herself in the magazine, he might even return to his seat.

* * *

There was a sound of tearing paper as she stared blindly at a paragraph which she had re-read several times without a glimmer of understanding. A dark, satiny box, smelling deliciously of rich chocolates, appeared from beneath its chrysalis of colored cellophane. He touched her gently on the arm.

"I hope you like these?"

She looked up, and was surprised by the kind intent she saw in his eyes. She was immediately embarrassed, and ashamed of her behavior. She was usually such a happy and even-tempered person yet, somehow, today she'd been less than that.

"Oh, yes. Thank you," she said, selecting a cream-colored truffle which was crisscrossed by marvelous stripes of dark chocolate. "I really love these." He had purchased the exact box which she'd convinced herself not to buy in the duty-free shop.

"Would you mind if I removed my jacket? It's beginning to get a bit warm."

Alana tried not to stare at the furious outgrowth of black hair on his chest which became visible as he removed his tie, undid the first two ivory shirt buttons, then slid out of the well-tailored jacket.

"Much better." He flexed his shoulders, and an almost uncontrollable frisson of awareness rippled through Alana in response. Her hand plunged, without invitation, into the box of pungent truffles. She grabbed two of them, and reflexively popped both into her mouth. The expression on Damian Collins's face showed that he was struggling very hard to keep a straight face.

Alana stared at him, her eyes daring him to laugh. She groped about quickly for something to say, and seized the most obvious thing.

"I'm . . . I'm usually not this . . . this . . ." The right word escaped her. "But I am a bit hungry. I missed my breakfast this morning, you see. I hope you don't mind?"

Damian waved a benevolent hand, and Alana knew that he was still laughing at her.

"Help yourself. I'm glad you like them."

She was saved the indignity of having to explain her actions further by the start of the first-class cabin service. Struggling with the residual lump of chocolate in her mouth, she managed to explain to the flight attendant that, no, she would not like any wine and, yes, a glass of water would be nice.

The water came and she drank thirstily.

"More candy?" He proffered the box, and there were laughter lines beginning to crinkle his eyes.

From behind the long fluted glass of golden wine he held before him, she could see the beginnings of a smile. The humor of the situation suddenly struck Alana, and she dissolved into helpless laughter. Between giggles, she said, "OK. OK. I can tell you want to get it out of you. You have my permission. Go ahead."

He chuckled heartily. "That poor woman could barely understand a single word you were saying."

Alana nodded, a huge grin on her face. "Our entire association has been a disaster from start to finish. Maybe we should quit while we're ahead, before something really awful happens."

"What else could happen?" Damian leaned back in his seat. "Alana Britton. Tell me about yourself."

And after a moment of hesitation, she did, but cautiously. Some inner reserve told her not to reveal anything too very personal. She told him about Oxford University, and what it'd been like studying there.

"It's really a wonderful old institution," she said, and her eyes were full of earnest enthusiasm. "My father studied there in the sixties. Growing up, he was always telling me all sorts of wonderful stories about the Oxford culture. Funny things about campus life. The rivalry between Oxford and Cambridge. The cricket matches . . ."

Damian's eyebrows rose a fraction. "Don't tell me you were involved in those?"

Alana gave him a saucy smile. "Why not? Women play baseball in the U.S., don't they?" She had guessed, a little earlier, because of the noticeable twang, that he was an American.

Damian nodded. "Well . . . not professionally."

Alana waved that piece of information aside and charged on. "Anyway, cricket is very similar to baseball, and it's loads of fun." She picked up her paper napkin and tore it into little pieces. "Here. I'll show you what I mean."

She wadded the pieces into little balls, then arranged them strategically on her tray table. "This is the basic layout of a cricket field." She pointed to the wads of paper and, for the next several minutes, carefully explained the intricacies of the game. When she was through, there was an expression of genuine admiration on Damian's face.

"I never would have figured you for a sports fan. I guess you must've been a terrible tomboy growing up."

Alana nodded, and there was a trace of nostalgia in her eyes. "I was. Most of the time, something was either bruised or bleeding. My poor mother just gave up on me after a while." Alana laughed. "I remember my Dad saying to her once 'Don't worry, she'll grow out of it.' "

Damian looked directly at her. "But you haven't, of course, since you're still whacking balls around and flinging yourself in the mud to make 'outs'."

Alana helped herself to another truffle and, this time, nibbled on it daintily. "I believe in having fun."

He smiled, and there was a wicked glint in his eyes. "That's good to know."

She shot him a sideways glance. He was extremely flirtatious, but in a charming way. She'd have to be careful with him, though. She didn't want to give him the wrong impression about her. She should probably talk about something more clinical. A subject less prone to double entendre.

Damian helped her considerably when he asked, "So. Did you go into the law like your dad?"

Alana pounced on the subject gladly. "No. . . ." She hesitated to tell him about Harry. She really didn't want to divulge too many personal tidbits about her life. "I went into science."

"A doctorate?"

"Yes," she nodded, and she found herself talking easily about the program which she had just completed, regaling him with amusing incidents which had often occurred during the practical labs. Damian laughed heartily at many points in the story. Hours passed without her really realizing it, and soon she was no longer talking about the University. He had wanted to know about Guyana and what it was like there, so she told him. Every last detail she could scrounge up. She made sure she gave him the interesting tidbits too, those which would never be found in a travel guide. He listened with rapt attention and didn't even seem to notice that she told him little or nothing about what her life there was really like. He just let her talk, nodding a lot, and, occasionally, nudging her in one conversational direction or another. By lunchtime, she had decided that he was really quite a nice person after all, even if he didn't say much about himself.

She fell asleep for several hours after lunch. When she awoke the seats beside her were empty, but someone had covered her with a warm blanket and lowered the window shades. She glanced at her watch, then pulled up the shutter to take a look at the sky. It was almost dark.

"How much longer to Piarco?" she asked a passing flight attendant.

The woman looked at her watch. "Not very much longer now. We should be in Trinidad in . . . a little over three hours. Can I get you anything to drink? Another pillow, maybe?"

"Nothing, thanks," Alana said. She swung her feet up onto the seat and really settled into a comfortable position. She drew the blanket up under her chin, closed her eyes, and, in the darkness, thought foolish, romantic thoughts about Damian Collins. She knew that none of it could ever be possible, of course. They came from such different worlds. Not to mention the fact that they were also on their way to different countries. It was nice just to imagine though . . . just to imagine. She was asleep again within minutes.

She awoke as they began their descent into Piarco International Airport. Damian was shaking her gently.

"We'll be landing in a few minutes," he said. "Hope you're a lot better at landings than you are takeoffs."

Alana sat up. She rubbed a fist across her eyes as a child would, then she favored him with a grin. "Oh, I love landings. There's something comforting about seeing land just below. Knowing that the wheels are down . . . waiting . . . then the bump, as we touch the tarmac . . . the screeching of rubber against asphalt . . . it's the best part of the flight for me."

Damian snapped the belt head into the buckle and pulled the strap low and tight across his lap. "You make it sound so . . . exciting." He gave her a pensive look, hesitated for a moment, then asked, "Sure I can't convince you to spend the week in Trinidad with me?"

Alana blinked at him for a moment. She had thought that they had successfully gotten past all that. That they were almost friends now.

"No. I'm sorry. . . . I couldn't." Her eyes met his and, for a brief moment, they held. Damian reached out a hand and ran the back of an index finger down the length of her cheek. His skin felt coarse and nubby, like raw silk. Black eyes looked directly into hers, and Alana felt something deep and primal stir within her.

"I guess this is good-bye, then." He unsnapped his seat belt and stood, looking down at her. "I'm sorry we didn't have more time."

"Yes. We could've . . . talked more."

He smiled, and Alana knew that talking wasn't exactly what he'd had in mind. She watched him walk back to his seat, then turned her head to look at the pinpoints of light as they appeared below. As she stared down into the vast darkness, her thoughts returned to the man seated several rows in front of her. She wondered if picking up women this way was normal for him. He was certainly handsome enough to pull it off easily. Not very many women would turn him down. Though he should have realized, after spending so many hours talking to her, that she would never have agreed to spend the week with him.

So fierce was her concentration that it was a second or two before the full import of what was being said really struck her. There was going to be a slight delay on the ground. Nothing to worry about. Just refueling and a standard maintenance check. Ongoing passengers were being urged to disembark and stretch their legs.

Alana let out a tight little breath. If she were a superstitious person, she would think that she'd been hexed.

Once the plane had taxied to a stop, the lights in the cabin came on, and the plane erupted into life. A toddler, disturbed by the activity, began screaming in earnest as his harassed mother attempted to subdue him and manage her carry-on luggage at the same time. Alana reached up a hand and pressed her call button.

"About how long will this delay be?" she asked the flight attendant.

"Oh, no more than half an hour or so . . . until we get clearance to be on our way again. Why don't you get off and have a look around Piarco Airport? Pick up a few souvenirs?"

Alana glanced at her watch. Harry was probably already on his way to Timehri. She'd have to call him and let him know that she would be late getting in.

The first class passengers were let off first. Alana slung her jacket across an arm and moved forward. Damian Collins stepped aside so that she might exit first. She gave him a polite smile and walked briskly ahead. She was aware that he was only a few steps behind, and this caused her to hurry even more. She spied a bank of phones as she entered the airport, and she walked across to them. She watched Damian Collins walk by the glass cubicle. He nodded to her as they made eye contact. Alana watched until he was out of sight, then she punched in the number to Harry's private extension. She knew that her brother was going to be surprised to hear from her, since she was, at this very minute, supposed to be en-route.

Her eyes glowed with enthusiasm as the phone began to ring. It had been such a very long time. Harry had also gone to Britain. He had chosen to study law at Cambridge instead of at Oxford. He had completed his law degree two years before Alana had finished her doctorate. But they had written each other long, detailed letters, and run up huge telephone bills talking until the wee hours of the morning. Harry was more than just her brother, he was her best friend, her champion, her protector. Although they were separated by only two years, Harry had grown quickly and matured early. By age eighteen, he stood well over six feet, dwarfing his petite sister. He was very athletic, and handsome enough that he could have made a solid career for himself as a professional model. When they went out together, Alana was always amused by the envious glances that were cast her way by other women. Harry thoroughly enjoyed the attention, of course, and Alana always had enormous fun, teasing him about his narcissistic ways. Just thinking about it brought a smile to her face.

After about two minutes of consistent ringing, Alana was on the verge of hanging up, when, without warning, the ringing ceased, and a deep voice said, "Britton."

"Harry," she said, and her voice sparkled. "Where were you? I've been ringing for ages."

"Lani! You can't be at Timehri yet."

"I'm not," she said, hugging the phone close.

"Is something wrong . . . look, where are you?" There was immediate concern in his voice.

"I'm at Piarco. I'm talking to you from a phone booth in the airport."

"You weren't supposed to get off. What're you doing there?"

"They asked us to disembark for a little while. They said half an hour. It's probably nothing."

"Sure?"

"Sure."

"OK, then. I'll be waiting for you in the lounge area, so hurry up and get here. I can't wait to see you."

She laughed happily. "I'll try. And Harry?"

"Yes?"

"I love you."

She heard his deep chuckle. "I love you too, Shorty."

Alana hung up, took a deep breath, then stepped outside the cubicle. She'd try the duty-free shops again.

She spent the next twenty minutes wandering around from store to store, listening all the while for her flight's boarding call. She bought some Trinidadian carvings, a small wicker basket with funny little figures painted on the sides, a key chain for her father, a pair of filigree silver earrings for her mother, and a stack of tee-shirts with different Trinidadian slogans printed on the front. She bought two of each color. Harry would love the ones she had chosen for him.

After nearly half an hour, she checked with the airline desk clerk, and was told that there was no problem, and that an announcement would soon be made. She browsed the shops for a bit longer, then finally sank into a chair to wait. Her feet were tired and, although she had slept for a few hours on the plane, she couldn't wait to get home to a nice soft bed.

When the announcement came, she was half asleep. She listened in disbelief. Her flight had been postponed until the next day because of mechanical difficulties. All passengers were being asked to check with Customs before going to the baggage claim area.

What ensued thereafter was nothing short of complete chaos. There was one man at the Customs desk handling a long line of very irate passengers. The line weaved from side to side as people pushed and shoved, some shouting at the tops of their voices, threatening the man at the desk with everything from bodily injury to lawsuits. A rather odious man, tightly buttoned into a straining polyester suit, was the most vocal of the lot. And he somehow managed to whip the crowd into an even greater frenzy.

"Is where we gon' sleep tonight, eh? I done pay me money to Timehri. We in't eat nuttin' fuh hours. Not even a piece a' dry bread. Y'all playin' wid me? I gon' bus' somebody backside tonight!"

Then he turned to a thin, bespectacled man who was being sandwiched between a large woman and himself, and asked in a voice dripping with menace, "Is where you shovin' going? You must t'ink you's royalty."

By the time Alana had managed to make it to the Customs desk, she was hot, harassed, and on the verge of slapping the rotund man in the polyester suit. She got through the formalities quickly and hurried off to find her luggage. She thanked heaven for her decision to travel light. Since she was returning home for good, most of her things had been sent ahead in trunks.

A short while later, she stood at the conveyor belt in a crush of people, straining to see if her bag had come off yet. She spied a thick black suitcase and elbowed her way to the front of the crowd. Mr. Polyester was there again.

"Is where de luggage deh?" he bellowed in Alana's ear. "Wha' de rass is dis?"

Alana pounced on her bag just as another hand also descended on it. She tugged, all vestiges of decorum gone. The clasp holding the hair off her face gave way at that precise moment, and her hair spilled forward in corkscrew jet ringlets. She was aware that she must look like a wild Amazon, but couldn't have cared less. This was her suitcase, and she refused to let go of it.

"Miss," the voice at her side said sharply. "This is my case. Now let go before you hurt yourself."

Alana looked up through a mass of hair. There were beads of perspiration standing out visibly on her nose. With the way things had been going, she wasn't at all surprised to discover the identity of the person with whom she was doing battle. Damian Collins.

"God, I must be in some kind of karmic spiral," she muttered. "What are you doing here?"

"Good Lord." He seemed quite shocked. "It's Alana Britton. What has happened to you?"

She raised a trembling finger. "Please . . . please do not ask me that question. It would take hours. I'm not even sure that I could explain it. Why are you still here, anyway?"

He released his grip on the suitcase. "There was some delay in getting the luggage off. Then a bit of confusion about where the luggage was."

Alana gave a mighty heave and removed the suitcase from the conveyor belt. She hardly noticed when her right shoe heel snapped off. She hobbled away from the crowd, dragging the suitcase with her. There was a bright determination in her eyes. She had to try to see the positive side of things. She did have her clothes and toiletries, after all. And, very soon, she'd be in some nice quiet hotel where she'd be able to take a long hot bath, have a meal, and then go right off to bed. Things were improving, indeed.

Damian came up behind her. He was carrying an identical bag.

"You know, I really think you have my bag; you see, it has a . . ."

"I think I'm still capable, despite all that has happened to me today, of recognizing my own luggage," Alana snapped. She apologized almost immediately. "I'm sorry. I guess my temper is a bit frayed."

"Well, by the looks of you, I'd say that you'd been through a lot." He smiled. "I won't hold it against you."

Alana was in no mood to be charmed. "Which hotel are we supposed to be going to?" She forgot for a second that Trinidad was actually his destination, and that he was not involved in the layover confusion.

He appeared almost regretful when he asked, "Didn't you hear the announcement? Everywhere's booked up."

"What?" Alana stuttered. This was the limit.

"It's always like this around Christmas time, I've heard. I guess you'll just have to sleep in the lobby of the Ambassador. I think everyone else is going to do that." He directed a pensive look in her direction. "You should be safe, though. There'll be lots of people around."

Alana took a deep breath, then expelled it slowly. "Oh no. No, no sir. I am not sleeping in the lobby of the Ambassador or anywhere else." She brushed the hair back from her face, and succeeded in making an even wilder mess of it. "I'm going to insist that they give me a room. They'll have to."

The corner of his mouth twitched and, for a brief moment, Alana felt certain that he was going to laugh. She stared directly into his eyes, daring him even to chuckle. His face was a little too serious when he asked, "Would you like some help with that bag?"

Alana lifted her head and, with as much dignity as she could muster, said, "I can manage."

"Come with me, then." There was a flash of something very like admiration on his face. "We'll see if anything can be worked out with the Hyatt. They're usually pretty accommodating there."

Alana followed him slowly, limping along in her shoes. He adjusted his pace so that she could keep up.

"Why not take the shoes off altogether?" he asked, after observing her limping gait.

She responded with a very determined shake of her head. "Thank you, but I'll keep them on, if it's quite all right with you."

She thought she might have heard him laugh, then, but couldn't be sure since they were now outside, and competing with the noises of the street.

They took a taxi across to the hotel and were greeted with a similar situation of chaos. There were people slouched in chairs, huddled on the floor, and milling aimlessly around. The general din was so great that Alana almost collapsed right there. The undamaged heel on her other shoe wobbled dangerously as she attempted to balance herself and the suitcase adequately. She felt certain that Damian Collins was laughing again, but she wouldn't turn to see. Instead, she lifted her chin and hobbled up to the front desk. There was no one in sight, so she banged on the bell. It took a couple of minutes for a desk-clerk to appear. After a session of hollering, she was told that she could rest in the manager's office for the remainder of the night. She thanked the flustered clerk very politely and turned to retrieve her bag. Damian was still there.

"Any luck?" he asked.

Alana took a deep, calming breath. How did he manage to look so cool and handsome amidst all this confusion?"

"I have the manager's office for the night."

A smile danced in his eyes. "Why spend an uncomfortable night in an office when you can stay upstairs in my suite?"

Alana's eyes misted over with gratitude. "You mean

you'd really sleep down here and let me have your suite?"

His lips curled upwards in a little smile. "I meant, you might share it with me."

"Oh." Understanding dawned in a quick thrust. For a moment she had forgotten what kind of a man he was. It was so easy to forget. So easy to like him and to let her guard down.

She titled her head up. "I'm sorry; I couldn't."

"Why not?" he pressed. "We're both adults."

Afterwards she could have bitten her tongue. But it was out before she had a chance to really evaluate the wisdom of her words.

"For the simple reason that I'm . . . I'm married," she said a little wildly, and then cringed inside at the lie. She could have said anything at all: *That he was a stranger. That it would be decidedly unwise to do such a thing. Anything.*

Alana stood staring at him, looking not unlike a petrified deer trapped in the headlights of an oncoming vehicle. His hand tightened on the handle of the suitcase, and an unreadable expression settled on his face.

He stared at her for several seconds without saying a word. Alana wondered if the lie was there on her face for him to see. Did it show, that she was an innocent, and could never have been married at any time? She found herself praying that he would believe her. That he would turn around and walk away without questioning her any further.

"Well," he said finally, "your husband is a very lucky man."

Alana said several quick prayers of thanks, and stretched her lips into a polite smile.

He turned to go, then paused. "If you need to tidy up a bit, I'm in the presidential suite. Stop by if you need anything."

Watching him walk away, Alana felt absolutely rotten. She must be getting soft in the head. Since meeting Damian Collins, she had stammered like an idiot, crushed his instep, gobbled handfuls of chocolates in the most unladylike fashion, and now this . . . this horrible lie. She was twenty-six years old, for heaven's sake. Certainly old enough to say "no" to a man in a calm and dignified fashion.

She bent to get the case at her feet, then half dragged, half lifted it into the manager's office and collapsed onto a large sofa. This had been one of the worst days of her life. From start to finish, she had made a complete fool of herself. She just thanked heaven that she had a plain gold ring that she could slip onto her left hand. It was a trifle more narrow than the traditional band, but it would suffice, in the off chance that she saw Damian Collins again. She had no intention of taking him up on his invitation to "tidy up" in his suite but, until tomorrow, when she was again safely on a plane out of Trinidad, the ring would remain on her finger.

After resting for a few minutes, she removed the key from her purse and bent down to fiddle with the lock. The hair kept falling into her eyes. She brushed it back, jiggled the lock again, then sat up and impatiently scraped the curly locks into a haphazard knot and secured them at the base of her neck. Before returning to her task, she removed her shoes and dug her toes into the soft pile carpet. Her feet were sore and tired, and just wiggling her toes around a bit caused some of the tension to ease. It was heavenly. A frown suddenly puckered her smooth forehead. Dear God: Harry. He'd be waiting at Timehri Airport in Guyana. She glanced at her watch and groaned. He was probably already there. She would have to call him, tell him what had happened. But not before she changed into some comfortable shoes.

She lifted the suitcase up so that it was standing instead of lying flat. What was the matter with the darn lock, anyway? She stuck the key in again, gently this time, then gave it a sharp turn clockwise. It took a full minute of very vigorous jiggling for her to accept that the key could not open the lock. She straightened up and sat unmoving as realization slowly hit her. It was his suitcase. He'd been right all along. Her eyes watered with self-pity. Why was fate conspiring against her? What had she done? She wiped a tear of frustration away and stood up. She would have to go up to his suite after all.

A few minutes later, Alana stood outside the presidential suite. It appeared to take up more than half of the entire top floor of the hotel. She took a deep breath, then pounded on the door. She made a silent resolution. There would be a minimum of talk. Regardless of how charming he was, she would just collect her suitcase and leave.

The door swung open almost immediately. He was dressed in a black hotel robe that gaped open from the neck to the waist, and was loosely belted across the hips. The profusion of black hairs which she had noticed on the plane was now revealed in its full glory. They curled thick and silky across the entire expanse of his chest, tapering to a thin line which disappeared at the point where the robe came together.

Alana felt her entire body respond to him. She could tell that he felt something, too, because his gaze narrowed, and a muscle twitched at the corner of his jaw. Her throat went dry, then hot. And for a minute they just stood there, not saying anything.

"You were right about the suitcase," she finally managed.

He did not respond as she had expected him to. There were no "I told you so's." Instead, he stood aside and motioned for her to enter. This was not the way she had envisioned it.

"Oh . . . there's no need. What I mean is . . . I really don't have to come in; I just want my suitcase."

He touched her gently on the arm, and again there was that kindness in his eyes which she had noticed on the plane.

"Come on in," he said softly, "you look half dead." He stood aside and motioned for her to enter. When she hesitated, he said, "It's all right. I've never had to force myself on a woman."

Alana met his eyes directly. They were clear eyes. Eyes you could trust. And, in this light, she could see that they were actually black, and not a very dark brown, as she had thought. She took a breath and decided.

"OK. But just for a minute. I am really tired."

He closed the door behind her and the lock made a solid thunk as it clicked into place.

Alana took a quick glance around the massive suite. It was luxuriously appointed, but she hardly noticed that. Her eyes went directly to the dishes of food set neatly on a small dining table. She realized that she was hungry; very hungry.

"Come on in and have a seat," he said. "I ordered dinner for you."

Alana's eyes darted back to him. "You ordered . . . for me? How did you know I would . . . ?"

He gave her a patient smile and waved her into a chair, which was already pulled out from the table.

"You did have my suitcase."

"Yes . . . well, I'm sorry about that. I guess I should've listened to you at the airport. But with everything else all happening at once . . . all the confusion . . . the shouting . . . pushing. I couldn't even hear myself think."

He unfolded two white linen napkins and handed her one. His fingers brushed lightly over hers, and she immediately sat back in the chair.

"Are you this nervous around all men"—his eyes took on a seductive glitter—"or is it just me?"

Alana ignored the taunt. This had not been a good idea. Her original plan of getting the suitcase and leaving immediately had been much better. She would just give Harry a call, grab a couple of bread rolls, thank Damian Collins nicely for the dinner she wasn't going to eat, and then retire to the manager's office for the rest of the night. With that decision made, she felt stronger, more able to fight off the primitive signals his body was sending out.

She gave him a firm look. "I'd like to make a call if I could."

He nodded. "Of course. But why don't you eat first? You look about ready to pass out."

It was her turn to give the patient smile. "First I call, then I eat." Alana was proud of how sturdily she had said that.

She had expected an argument out of him but, instead, he pointed to a phone tucked away in the corner of the room. "Do you know how to dial out?"

Alana nodded. She hoped that he would leave the room while she was on the phone. She couldn't possibly make the call with him sitting there listening to every word she said to her nonexistent "husband." Not to mention what Harry would think if she was forced to refer to him as "darling," or "sweetheart."

Damian seemed to understand her desire for privacy, for he pushed back the chair and stood. "I'll go fetch your suitcase and change into something more suitable."

Alana gave him a grateful smile. Once he had left the room and she was sure the door was closed, she dialed quickly. A few minutes later when he returned, she was finished with her call. He had changed into a pair of cream slacks and a loose-fitting black cotton shirt. He glanced at her briefly.

"Everything settled?"

She nodded. "Yes." Her call to Harry had gone straight to his car phone. She had left a message with the chauffeur. Her eyes followed him now as he walked across to the front door and placed her suitcase directly in front of it.

She was thinking about how she might politely tell him that she would not be staying for dinner after all when he leaned forward and said, "Look, I want to apologize for that little comment I made earlier. I realize that it could have made you feel a bit uncomfortable . . . you being a married woman and all. I wouldn't blame you if you decided that you couldn't have dinner with me. . . ."

He began taking the lids off dishes and spooning fragrant rice and other niceties onto separate plates.

"Still," he continued in the most companionable fashion, "you must be hungry. So why don't you have something to eat? And, if you prefer, I won't say a word."

He placed a very full plate before her. Again there was that pulling smile in his eyes. "You know, I'm really not such a bad guy."

Alana felt her lips curving upward. She wondered if he was a salesman by profession. If he wasn't, she felt that he certainly should be. To anticipate her response, and then to neatly put her in a position where it would be hard to refuse him without seeming boorish, was certainly talented. And he did it so easily, and with such charm. A solitary dimple appeared in her right cheek, and her eyes glowed at him with amusement and the beginnings of something deeper.

"I was going to excuse myself."

He nodded as though it was no surprise to him. "Am I forgiven?"

Alana's lips stretched into a huge smile, and he returned it.

"You're very hard to refuse."

He laughed then. And Alana decided that he had a very nice laugh. It was a deep, husky rumble that started somewhere deep down in his chest. It was a warm sound that somehow made her think of fireplaces, dim lights, and bubbling glasses of golden champagne.

"I wasn't sure what you would like," he said, pointing to the many silver dishes, "so I ordered a little of everything. Some rice with . . . red beans. Curried beef. Steamed chicken. Sweet potatoes. A green salad. Cream soup. Strawberry sorbet . . . Have a look; there's more. I hope I chose something you like."

They ate, mostly in silence since Alana was ravenous and also not very anxious for any discussion about her nonexistent marriage. She put away the entire plate of food which Damian had dished, including a slice of pie for dessert and a healthy topping of ice cream. Somewhere near the conclusion of the meal she became aware that he had stopped eating and was instead observing her with great interest.

She felt a flush of embarrassment on her cheeks. Here she was, making a complete pig of herself. Probably the only thing she hadn't done was grunt and make little oinking noises over her food. She dabbed the corners of her mouth with the linen napkin.

"I hadn't realized how very hungry I was."

His hand moved toward hers as though he intended to touch her again—then, abruptly, it stopped, as though he'd just remembered that he couldn't.

"You were hungry," he said instead. "Besides, it's much better to eat well than to pick at your food."

"Let me help clear up a bit, then I'll be off to my couch downstairs." She tried to joke.

"I've been meaning to talk to you about that. This suite has two massive bedrooms; why don't you just stay up here . . . ?"

"Oh . . . no, no. I mean, it has nothing to do with you personally. I'm sure you're a . . ." She struggled to find the appropriate word. She wasn't at all certain that he was trustworthy. He was nice, of course, but then again she was certain that Jack the Ripper must have been "nice" too. If he hadn't been, it would have been a trifle more difficult for him to prey on so many unsuspecting women.

"The bedroom door has a key. You could lock that, if it would make you feel more secure."

The idea appealed to her for a second. A warm bed, as opposed to a hard, lumpy couch . . . and after such a grueling journey, too. And it would be nice to have a hot shower, to change into some fresh clothes. But she couldn't. She knew nothing at all about this man. How could she remain in the same room as he . . . overnight?

He watched her struggle through the options. As she opened her mouth to refuse again, he said, "All right. You can have the suite for tonight. I'll take the couch downstairs. But on one condition": He raised a finger as she was about to speak again. "Tomorrow, you come with me for a quick tour around Port-of-Spain."

"But . . . I'm leaving tomorrow."

He shoved both hands into his pockets, and stood

relaxed before her. "Do you know yet what time you're leaving?"

"They said to be at the airport no later than two P.M."

"Good. So if we start out at, say, seven o'clock, we could more than adequately explore the city before you need to head for the airport. Port-of-Spain is a very interesting city, I've heard. What do you say?"

She laughed. "Are you in sales?"

He grinned at her. "Seven o'clock tomorrow then?"

She nodded. "It's splendid of you to let me have the suite. How can I thank you?"

He gave her an audacious wink. "I'll think of something."

He opened the door. "And forget about clearing up. Housekeeping will take care of it in the morning."

Later, after taking a long hot shower and a brush to her hair, Alana lay in bed thinking of the man sleeping on the couch downstairs. After a while, she closed her eyes. She wouldn't feel guilty about turning him out of his own suite. It would only be for one night, anyway. And, maybe at some future point, she might be able to return the favor. She'd think of some way. Some small thing she could do. Maybe if he was ever in Guyana . . . In minutes, she was asleep and dreaming.

Two

The insistent ringing of the telephone on the bedside table woke her the next morning. For a few seconds she looked around, disoriented; then everything came back at once. She glanced at her watch and sprang out of bed. It was already six-thirty. She snatched the phone up.

"Hello?"

"Thought I'd give you a wake-up call. Also, I'd like to take a shower. Mind if I come up?"

"Oh, yes . . . sure, come on up." Her eyes flew around the room. She was always a very neat person. But last night she'd felt so very tired that she hadn't had the energy to clear up after herself.

"I'll be up in five minutes, OK?"

"That's fine."

She replaced the phone in the cradle. In a few minutes, she had picked up and neatly folded away her garments of the day before. She was in the bath vigorously lathering herself when she heard the front door open and close. She turned the volume of the shower down a bit so that she could listen better to the footsteps on the parquet flooring. They were headed away from her bedroom. She turned the shower up again to rinse off.

* * *

A few minutes before seven, she was ready. She emerged from the bedroom dressed in a crumple-free midnight-blue jumpsuit. Her mane of blue-black hair cascaded in bouncy ringlets about her shoulders. She wore a minimum of makeup, never having needed the elaborate concoctions of powders and creams which were used to ensure a smooth blemish-free complexion. The healthy glow about her was one of the first things Damian noticed as she entered the room. She gave him a beautiful smile and a bright "Good morning."

"Had a good night?"

Alana was ridiculously pleased by the frank admiration in his eyes. Her pleasant temperament had been completely restored by the night's rest, and she was ready to face whatever challenges lay before her.

"Very good. Was the couch very uncomfortable?"

"I've slept on much worse. It took a bit of explaining to the management, of course, but I was finally able to convince them that I hadn't done away with you. Before we leave this morning, they would like it very much if you reassured them of your safety."

He rose to his feet and stood with hands in pockets, towering over her. There was a new expression in his eyes, one which Alana found difficult to interpret. There was a smattering of humor, tolerance, and something else.

"I'm sure you'll thank God when I get onto the plane this afternoon. I've been a terrible burden to you. You've been so very nice about it, too. Let me buy you breakfast? It's the least I can do," she said as he began to object.

His big shoulders moved up and down in a quick shrug. "OK. If it'll make you feel better."

Alana nodded. "It will."

"Why don't we eat somewhere outside the hotel

then? Some small Trinidadian place with lots of local color?"

Alana smiled. "All right. Just let me grab my purse." She disappeared and was back within seconds.

"We'll walk for a bit, then maybe rent a car to explore the outskirts. Sound OK?"

"Fine with me." Alana's eyes were bright and eager. She looked down at her shoes. "No heels this time, so your feet should be quite safe."

He laughed down at her, his eyes a deep, inky black. He stuck out his arm and, after a moment of hesitation, she took it. They went down in the elevator, still joking back and forth.

A quick stop was made at the manager's desk, where the man eyed Damian suspiciously, as though he wasn't quite convinced that everything was on the up and up.

"You're quite all right then, ma'am?"

"I'm fine," Alana said. "Mr. Collins was very kind and let me have his suite last night."

"Yes . . . ahh . . . Mr. . . . Collins did explain last night about the sleeping arrangements. It won't be necessary for anyone to sleep on the couch tonight, however. We now have several rooms available. I shall reserve one in your name—Miss . . . ?"

Alana took a deep breath. She had almost agreed with the man's assumption that she was a "miss." "Thank you very much, but that won't be necessary. I'm leaving for Guyana today."

The man smiled. "Enjoy your stay with us then. And you will come back to visit us soon?"

Alana assured him that she would. Damian asked for a visitor's guidebook of the city and asked about recommended sightseeing spots. The man handed over a small booklet, and gave several pieces of advice on which areas to avoid. Alana gave him a bright smile of thanks.

Outside, the sun was already very hot. It took a moment for Alana to become accustomed to the heat after the cool air-conditioning of the hotel.

"I'd forgotten how very hot it can be in this part of the world," Damian said.

Alana shielded her eyes with a hand and looked up at him. "Maybe you'd better buy a hat with a visor." She had already made up her mind not to question him about his life. She didn't want to know why he traveled as much as he appeared to. She didn't want to know anything about him, really. That way, he'd be much easier to forget.

Damian looked down at her from his considerable height. "What about you? I'm responsible for you until you get onto that plane this afternoon. I don't want you keeling over with sunstroke."

Alana grinned. "Sunstroke? Are you forgetting that I grew up with this kind of weather?"

His face took on an expression of mock sternness. "That may well be, missy, but we'll get one for you, too."

Alana shielded her eyes against the brilliant glare and looked around.

"Should we get a taxi, do you think?"

There were several cars parked at the curb with the letter "H" on their license plates. Damian gave them a quick look.

"Wouldn't it be more interesting to go on foot for a while instead of taking one of these hire cars?" He nodded toward one of the cars parked at the curb and the driver immediately got out and flung open the passenger door.

Alana chuckled quietly. "How're you going to get out of this? The man thinks you gave him some kind of secret signal."

Damian spoke to her through the corner of his mouth. "I'll just go over and explain that he misunderstood me. That I was, in fact, talking to you."

"Look, he's smiling at us. You can't disappoint him, Damian. We'll have to take him, now."

Damian looked down at her. "You softy."

Alana gave him a big grin, and something flared for an instant in his eyes.

"All right, all right, we'll ask him to take us to Independence Square. We can set out on foot from there."

The cabdriver waved them into the car, closed the door smartly behind, and set off at a rapid pace.

"You look like nice people," he began. "Honeymooners, eh?"

Before Alana could hastily deny his assumption, the man had galloped on to another topic. "Po't-A-Spain is de best damn little city in de wo'ld, you hear?"

Damian cleared his throat. "Yes, I've heard that. . . . Independence Square, please."

The cab driver continued as though Damian had not spoken.

"If you want to see Po't-A-Spain, I can show you Po't-A-Spain. Not de side the tourists usually see. I mean de real Po't-A-Spain. You eva' hear about Keith Dennis?" And the man turned completely in his seat to stare at his two passengers.

Alana was torn between marveling at the man's physical dexterity and genuinely fearing for her life. A maxitaxi whipped by them, crammed full of passengers, and Alana clutched at Damian's hand.

He held it and whispered in her ear. "Maybe we should ask him to stop. We could walk the rest of the way."

"I wonder if he has a license?" Alana whispered back.

"I'll ask him." Damian leaned forward.

Alana gave him a pinch on the arm. "No," she said between giggles. He laughed back at her, his eyes sparkling with deep humor.

The taxi driver seemed completely unaware of the cause of their amusement.

"Keith Dennis is de best damn calypsonian in de wo'ld, you hear? If I took you down Lookout way, he would just take one look at you and write a song. Just like that. Just look at you and write a song." He peered at them through his rear view mirror. "All you eva' had shark and bake?"

"No." Damian and Alana shook their heads in unison.

The man peered at them in the rearview mirror again. "If you eat nothing else in life, you have to taste a shark and bake. It good, you hear?"

"Well, sometime later . . . maybe," Damian began.

"Maybe, nothing. I can take you there right now. I know de people. Good friends of mine up Maracas way. Shark meat is de sweetest meat, you hear? De best in de wo'ld."

"We really just want to go to Independence Square for now," Alana said. "We haven't had breakfast yet and . . ."

"All you want something simple to eat?" And he turned in his seat again, taking his eyes completely off the road.

"Well . . . yes," Alana began.

"Good. I'll take you up to de Savannah. They got good food there, you hear?"

Alana looked across at Damian. He was laughing quietly.

"You're not helping at all," she said. A little smile was beginning to curve the corners of her lips.

He shrugged. "Seems like we're prisoners. It might be better to just sit back and enjoy the scenery."

"At least we're getting a good look at Port-of-Spain," Alana agreed. She glanced out the window. The streets were narrow, and bustling with vehicular and pedestrian traffic. Every so often, someone would sound a car horn, lean out a window, and swear loudly at a bicyclist riding unconcernedly in the middle of the road.

Alana cranked the window down a bit more. "Everyone seems in a terrible hurry to get somewhere."

"Uhmm," Damian agreed. "I'd heard that Port-of-Spain was one of the busiest little cities in the Caribbean, but I didn't expect it to be quite this busy."

After a few minutes, they turned off the main street and onto one which was wider and not as heavily trafficked.

"The houses along this road are quite large, aren't they?" Alana said, pointing to a rather spacious-looking white Victorian.

Damian leaned closer. "They look like estate houses. What's this street called?" he asked the driver.

"Pembroke."

The man was about to turn around again and Damian patted him on the shoulder. "It's OK," he said, "you don't have to keep turning around whenever we say something."

The man met Damian's eyes in the mirror, and he grinned good-naturedly. "It takes a little time to get used to the way we drive here in T&T. But don't worry. I'll drive nice and slow for you. I know all the right spots to take you and your wife."

Alana took this opportunity to pipe up. "Well . . . we're not marri . . ."

But the taxi driver didn't give her a chance to finish. "You eva' hear about Carnival?" he asked.

Damian whispered to Alana. "It's no use. Maybe he's hard of hearing or something."

"Or something," Alana agreed.

"Carnival is de best bacchanal in de whole damn wo'ld, you hear? Better than carnival in Rio, or Mardi Gras in New Orleans. You can't hear no better calypso in the whole wo'ld like you hear at Carnival time in Po't-A-Spain. I could tell you some things about Carnival in Po't-A-Spain, you hear? Things you wouldn't believe. You know de Savannah? De same place we're going now? Well, de real name is Queens Park but all we Trinis call it de Savannah. At Carnival time, all de calypso caravans compete there. You eva' hear about the Mighty Sparrow? Or Lord Larro? They're some of de best damn calypsonians in the whole wo'ld you hear?"

"What about Crazy, or Black Stalin?" Alana asked. She was beginning to warm to the conversation, having realized that there was no point in trying to get the taxi driver to go where they wanted him to.

"Crazy and Stalin? They good, you hear? They're some of the best damn calypsonians in the wo'ld. You like steel band music?" The man met Alana's eyes in the mirror.

She smiled at him. "I love it."

"I'll take you to a real steel pan yard after you eat at de Savannah."

Alana turned to Damian, her eyes shining. "Do you mind? I'd love to see what a real steel pan yard looks like."

He gave her a puzzled look. "You've never seen a pan yard? I thought you were supposed to have grown up in this part of the world."

She took a small breath before answering. "Not every West Indian has seen a steel pan yard. It's not as run-of-the-mill as you might think."

"What part of de West Indies are you from?" The driver was peering at Alana in the mirror again.

"Guyana," she said.

The driver nodded his head back and forth for a minute. "Guyana. De best damn little country in all of South America, you hear? De best damn little country. Don't worry about Brazil, or Venezuela. I know all about Guyana, you hear? Got lots'a relatives living there. Important people, too. You eva' met de Prime Minister of Guyana?"

Alana's breath halted in her throat for a brief minute. "Yes. As a matter of fact . . ."

The driver nodded. "I met him once, too. He came on a State visit to Trinidad a couple years ago."

She met the driver's eyes in the mirror. "Is that right?"

The driver suddenly pulled the car off the road and parked it close to one of several long flatbed trucks.

"This is de Savannah."

They were now in a large green park-like area. The driver sprang out with remarkable agility and rushed around to the left passenger door. He opened it with a flourish and helped Alana out. After Damian had exited, he closed the door.

"What all you like? I know de vendors here. They make de best damn food in all of Po't-A-Spain, you hear?"

Alana gave the truck a dubious glance. "Do you think we should?" she whispered to Damian. "It mightn't be hygienic."

Damian placed his arm beneath her elbow and maneuvered her forward. "Let's take a look. After all, they couldn't be selling here if they weren't approved vendors."

The taxi driver was speaking rapidly to one of the vendors, a tall skinny man with a machete in one hand. The skinny man beckoned to them.

"All you don't frighten. Come ova'."

The taxi man was anxiously pointing out dishes. "All you like omelet? It's done the Trinis' way. It's de best damn omelet in de wo'ld, you hear? Or what about some bake and cheese? Anyt'ing a t'all you want, you can have. Anyt'ing a'tall."

Alana and Damian spent several thoughtful minutes going over the many tasty selections which were all neatly housed in steaming silver dishes. After much consideration, Alana settled on a spicy cheese omelet done with several blends of cheese, hot peppers, green onions, and okra.

"Try a bake with that, mam," the taxi driver said, pointing to a round, very dense deep-fried bread. "These bakes are . . ."

This time, Alana cut him off. "I know, they're the best damn bakes in the whole world."

The taxi driver nodded in agreement. "The best damn bakes."

Damian came up behind her. He was carrying a plate stacked with a variety of Trinidadian niceties. The only thing he hadn't chosen were the bakes.

"Are you teasing our industrious friend?" he whispered in her ear.

Alana gave him an innocent look. "Me? Of course not. I was just agreeing with him."

Damian chuckled. "Come on; let's find a place to sit."

Alana took a quick glance around. "Oh, look. I think they're setting up a table for us under that tree over there." She took a deep breath, and her eyes sparkled at him. "I'm having a great time."

Damian took a hold of one of her arms. "Me, too."

The taxi driver met them under the tree. He pulled out a chair for Alana and waited until she was comfortably seated. Then he removed his cap to wipe his brow with a large floppy white handkerchief.

"It getting hot, eh?" He addressed his question to both his passengers. "Tall Boy!" He bellowed at the skinny young man with the machete. "Bring some water coconuts."

Within a couple of minutes, two long glasses with thick chunks of ice were placed on the table. Tall Boy dispensed the contents of first one, then the other, of the coconuts into the glasses. He placed the empty coconuts in a covered container close to the table.

"When all you finished, I'll come back and open up de coconuts for you." He smiled and gave a quick wink. "Dessert." Both he and the taxi driver retired to the shade of an awning set up next to the flatbed truck.

Damian looked at Alana; there was a smile in his eyes. "Well. Let's eat."

A soft breeze rustled through the leaves, making a hissing sound. Everything around was green and glistening with health. The scenery was gorgeous. Alana inhaled deeply. There was a sweet fragrance in the air. It could have been that of hibiscus flowers or any of a variety of other tropical plants. She smiled at Damian. "This is lovely, isn't it? And so peaceful, too."

"Uhmm," Damian agreed between mouthfuls. "The food isn't bad, either."

Alana cut a slice of omelet and a thick piece of bake. "I want to tell you. Nothing like this has ever happened to me before."

"You mean you're usually too busy to take time out to enjoy the simple things?"

"No . . . I mean, yes. . . . It's hard to explain."

He was chewing slowly, and regarding her with a faintly quizzical look.

"How long have you been married?" he asked suddenly.

Alana placed the delicious piece of omelet into her mouth, chewed thoroughly, and swallowed before making a reply. Her heart had started hammering at her ribs. Stupidly, she had hoped that he had forgotten all about her nonexistent marriage. She was no good at telling lies. She always thought of the most ridiculous things, like her being married, for instance. Now, she would have to start thinking of additional lies. More embellishments.

"Just a couple of years."

He nodded and looked away for a second, his interest caught by a brilliantly colored bird which swooped down close by to steal a crumb of bread. Alana took the opportunity to throw some more crumbs onto the grass, hoping to attract enough birds to further distract him.

"In Guyana, we call that one a Kiskadee," she said, pointing to a small bird with a yellow breast and sharp black beak.

"Uhmm," he said, and began to eat again.

Alana took a long drink from the wonderfully cool glass of coconut water. In less than five hours, she would never see Damian Collins again. Less than five hours. It wasn't such a very long time, after all. With some skillful prodding from her, it would be possible to keep him off the subject of marriage altogether.

"You're not eating."

Alana blinked at him for a second. She hadn't realized that he had been watching her. She looked across at his plate.

"Oh. You're all finished."

Damian leaned back in the chair and unbuttoned the first few buttons on his shirt. He gave her one of his expansive smiles. "It's a pity."

Alana placed the final forkful of omelet and bake into her mouth. "What is?"

"You, and me . . ."

Alana didn't let him finish. "It isn't often in life that you meet someone who . . . who you get along with so . . . so instantly. And it's nice to know that you're not one of those men who thinks that platonic relationships between males and females are impossible."

He laughed outright. "Thanks for putting me in my place."

Alana grinned at him. "Can't we just enjoy the city, and forget about everything else?"

He reached across to capture her hand, palm up. His thumb settled in the soft center, and paused for a moment to stroke slowly. The hairs on the back of Alana's neck stood at stiff attention, and she was tempted to pull her hand from within his.

"If you weren't married, Alana Britton, I'd show you exactly what my opinion is about platonic relationships. Tell me one thing though . . . do you love him?"

Her lungs felt so tight and constricted that she could hardly draw breath. "You mean . . . Har . . . Harry?"

"Is that his name? Doesn't have much character to it."

Alana removed her hand with a sharp jerk. "If you knew Harry, you wouldn't say so. And of course I love him."

"Why isn't he with you now? Is he too busy? Maybe he doesn't care enough?"

"That's . . ."

"I know. That's none of my business."

It wasn't what Alana had been about to say, but it would do just as well. He had made her feel defensive and protective toward her fictitious husband. And for him to suggest that Harry, her darling brother Harry, lacked character would have been ridiculous if it hadn't been so very funny.

"If you were mine . . ."

She stood up. How had the conversation taken this sudden turn? And why hadn't she chosen another name for her husband? When she told Harry about this, he would laugh for ages.

"Look," she said. Her tone was earnest, even a little prim. "I hope I haven't managed somehow to give you the wrong impression. I was just interested in seeing Port-of-Spain. Nothing else. I'm sorry if I misled you in some way."

He pushed back his chair and stood with his hands shoved down into his pockets. "I'm the one who should apologize. It's not often that you meet a"—he appeared to struggle for the word—"decent woman like yourself. But you're so very . . ." The word seemed to escape him again, and a muscle bulged and relaxed in his jaw. "Will you promise not to cut short our little tour if I promise to keep my mind away from non platonic subjects?"

Alana met his gaze directly. Somehow, it was impossible for her to remain upset with him for very long. He was such an irrepressible charmer.

"I'm not convinced that you could do that even if you tried."

"You don't know me very well. Friends?" He extended an arm.

Alana took his hand and pumped it solemnly. "All right. But I think we'd better sit back down. We're making the taxi man nervous."

"Maybe he thinks we're going to try and make a run for it."

"He'd probably chase us down, tackle us, and then drag us back into the car," Alana said.

Damian chuckled. "I wonder if all the taxi drivers down here are like this?"

Alana cast a quick glance over toward the long flatbed truck. "He's coming over. Get ready."

"All you finished?" The taxi driver panted as soon as he was close enough. The mid-morning sun and the unusual exertion had caused beads of perspiration to stand out on his forehead.

"It was a lovely meal," Alana said, smiling.

"The best damn meal," Damian added, and Alana held her breath so that she wouldn't laugh.

The taxi man smiled happily. "All you in't taste nothing yet. Wait til you have a big Trinidadian lunch. It good, you hear? You ready for dessert?"

Within minutes, the tall young man with the machete was back. With a couple of quick strokes, he cleaved the coconuts in half.

"To really enjoy it, all you have to eat it de Trinidadian way."

Damian looked on with great interest as the man cut a small piece from the husk of each coconut. "What are we going to do with those?" he whispered to Alana.

"Wait and see," Alana whispered back.

The small teardrop pieces of coconut husk were placed on the table next to each halved coconut. The tall young man grinned at Damian.

"These are de sweetest water coconuts in all'a Po't-A-Spain. It would be a crime to eat them with a silver spoon. You have to eat them with a spoon cut from de coconut husk. It even sweeter that way." He picked up one of the teardrop shaped pieces of husk and pantomimed what he meant.

"You use it just like a regular spoon, you see?" he said to both Alana and Damian.

Alana nodded. "We eat it exactly like this in Guyana, too."

"It's de best damn way to eat a coconut," the taxi driver nodded in agreement. "De best damn way."

* * *

At around ten o'clock, they set out again. Tall Boy waved them off with the gleaming machete. "All you come again soon, you hear?"

Alana promised him that they would, and waved to him through the back window of the taxicab until the lanky young man was out of sight.

The driver peered at them in the rearview mirror. "Where all you want to go now? The Botanical Gardens, or somewhere with real Trinidadian character."

Alana glanced at her watch. "We still have a bit of time. Why don't we go to the steel pan yard, then if we have enough time left over, we might . . . oh . . ."

Damian raised his eyebrows at her. "Oh, what?"

"Well . . . it's just that . . . well, there must be places that you want to see, too. I'm kind of taking over the direction of the entire tour . . . where we go and all that. Which places would you like to see? I mean really. Don't be polite. If you don't want to go to the pan yard, we can go anywhere at all that you'd prefer."

A slow smile slid into Damian's eyes, and his mouth twitched a bit at the corners.

"Has anyone ever told you that you're very regal? Is this what an Oxford education does for you?"

Alana smiled back at him. If she hadn't known that he was just teasing, she would have been a bit worried.

"Don't try to change the subject. Do you really want to go to the steel pan yard?"

He leaned closer so that the sun slanted across his face, emphasizing the inky blackness of his eyes.

"I'll go anywhere you want to go."

Alana blinked at him in surprise. She wasn't at all certain whether or not he was serious. She was glad that the taxi driver chose that very moment to resume his unique style of conversation.

Damian patted her hand and leaned closer to whisper, "We're friends, remember?"

He was so close that if Alana had turned her head just a fraction of an inch, the corner of her mouth would have touched his. She forced herself to take deep, even breaths. Quite suddenly, there didn't seem to be enough air in the taxicab.

"Could you open your window a bit more?" she croaked at Damian.

He shifted away from her to do as she asked, then turned to give her an unreadable look.

"Beginning to feel the heat, are you?"

Alana felt herself blush. What in God's name was the matter with her? It was an innocent comment, after all. He couldn't have intended her to read a double meaning into it. Surely? She gave him a dubious glance from out of the corners of her eyes. It was hard to tell what he was thinking even when he was looking directly at her. He had turned to look out the window in response to a comment which the taxi driver had just made about the denseness of traffic through Independence Square. He turned his head back toward Alana as she continued to look at him. It was as though he had felt her eyes on him.

"We don't have much time left."

Alana gave her watch a quick look. In about three hours she would have to head back to the hotel, pick up her luggage, then head off to the airport. She hadn't even known that this man existed before yesterday, so there was no reason, no reason at all to feel this strange sense of loss at the thought of maybe never seeing him again. She blinked hard and said in a cheery voice: "It's strange how very quickly the time seems to go when you're sightseeing."

Damian nodded. "What would happen if you decided to stay an extra day here?"

"Oh, no . . . I mean, I would have no reason to. If my flight arrived in Guyana without me on it, the . . .

I mean, Harry would be frantic. The panic and confusion it would cause would be just . . . just indescribable."

His jaw clenched for a moment and he turned back toward the window. The taxi driver babbled on happily; he appeared to be completely oblivious to the slight tension which had suddenly sprung up between his two passengers in the backseat.

"The steel pan yard I'm taking you to is de biggest in alla Po't-A-Spain. I know de owner. He's de best damn steel band player in alla Trinidad, you hear? De best damn steel band player."

Alana turned puzzled eyes away from Damian. She couldn't begin to understand the man.

"Do you think that the owner might give us a quick lesson on how to play the steel pans?" she asked the driver.

"Nothing would make him happier, mam. He can teach you everything you need to know in fifteen minutes. Give him an hour, and you'll be ready to play in de caravans at Carnival time."

"Sounds like fun, doesn't it, Damian?" In Alana's estimation, he was behaving rather like a spoilt little boy who had just been told that he had to go home from the fair a little earlier than planned. But she was determined to jolly him out of it.

He turned to give her a rueful look. There was a slight frown between his eyes. "I'm sorry. My mind was miles away. What were you saying?"

Alana felt a surge of irritation. So, if he couldn't bend her to his will, he was going to ignore her, was that it? Well, she wouldn't play along with him. She would show him that she wouldn't stoop to such childish behavior. She would be cheerful if it killed her.

"We were talking about the steel pan, and learning to play it."

The taxi driver repeated his boast about the owner of the steel pan yard, and Damian raised his eyebrows in response. "Sounds like quite a man."

"Don't be rude," Alana hissed at him. She had forgotten all about her vow of cheerfulness of only a scant minute before. "Because you're angry with me for some perverse reason of your own, that is no reason to take it out on our driver. He's such a pleasant man."

Damian laughed softly. "I bet, when you were a child, you were everyone's favorite person."

She didn't care to respond to his comment. He obviously saw her as a bleeding heart, someone who would stand up for and protect those who could not or would not do so themselves. And what was wrong with that, after all?

"Are we having a fight? Because I don't want to fight with you. I don't even understand what this is all about."

Damian leaned across and, before she could avoid him, he picked up her hand. "We are not having a fight. I just have an unusual sense of humor. Not everyone gets it."

He turned her palm over and studied it. The lines which crisscrossed it were long and sturdy. His index finger ran slowly down the flat of her palm. "A good long lifeline . . . and lots of love from a good man."

Alana peered at her hand. "Is that what you see? I see something else entirely."

Damian looked again. This time he allowed two fingers to creep onto her palm. "Wait a second . . . there's more. I see twelve, no, thirteen children. A large house in the country. Two dogs, four sheep, and a pet salamander."

Alana pulled her hand away, chuckling. "A salamander? Thirteen children? I hope you don't make your living as a psychic."

He grinned at her. "What's the matter, isn't the prediction to your liking?"

She gave him a wide smile in return. "Not entirely. I love children, of course. But I also want to do something meaningful with my life." She paused, then rushed on to add hastily, "not that having children isn't meaningful. I just . . . just need to make a worthwhile contribution to the world."

"You mean like discovering a cure for some dreaded disease?"

"If I did that, then, of course, that would be wonderful, but . . . it could be something smaller. If in some way I might help to push the envelope of scientific knowledge a little further . . . for the betterment of mankind."

"You're interested in doing research in chemistry then?"

"Yes. I'd love to. That's why I did a doctorate. But there are some complications. I might not be able to."

"Your husband?"

Alana met his eyes directly, and she gave a little internal sigh. So they were back to that again. And after they had been doing so well, talking about things that really mattered.

"Harry is all for whatever it is that I want to do."

"Then what's the problem?"

"It's hard to explain. I think I might start out teaching the subject. Then if the opportunity . . . oh, listen, do you hear that?" She was glad for the distraction.

Damian listened with her to the sweet tinkling sound that was getting louder by the minute.

"Steelband music!" Alana's eyes gleamed with excitement, and she leaned forward to tap the taxi driver on the shoulder.

"Is that music coming from the steel pan yard we're going to?"

The man beamed at her in the rearview mirror. "Yes, ma'am. Right now you're listening to some of Trinidad's finest. They practice here every day, sometimes for six to eight hours. The men playing are some of de best damn musicians in the wo'ld, you hear? De best damn musicians."

The driver pulled off the main road and made his way slowly to a rather ramshackle-looking gateway.

Alana leaned out the window, her eyes darting around with the enthusiasm of a child. The yard was strewn with rusted and half-painted oil drums, and there was an assortment of animals milling about. Amidst this confusion was a rather stately looking little building with wide double doors on three of its four sides. The front doors had been flung back so that sunlight flooded the very spacious interior. Alana could just make out several human shapes bent over rows and rows of steel pans.

"Can we just go in?" she whispered to Damian.

"Certainly, ma'am," the driver responded before Damian could answer. "They love visitors."

"They love visitors," Damian whispered in her ear.

Alana gave him a stern look. "Ssh."

The taxi driver pulled to a stop beneath a leafy mango tree. He bounded from the car and was at the right passenger door almost before the engine had stopped running.

He helped Alana out with the solicitious comment: "Watch your step, ma'am, there's cow filt' about."

Alana looked down at several heaping piles of cow dung. Behind her, she could hear the husky sounds of Damian's laughter. She maneuvered gingerly between the droppings. Nothing would spoil the beauty and excitement of this moment. She had always wanted to know what a real steel pan yard was like. Maybe this one was a bit rough around the edges but, no matter, the music more than made up for the slightly disheveled surroundings.

"Come on in, come on in." The taxi driver was at the door, waving them forward. He appeared to be completely unaware that his shoes were now caked with some nameless muck.

"Maybe I should carry you in," Damian muttered in her ear.

Alan giggled. "Or maybe I should carry you?"

A broad smile stretched his lips. "Right. And they'd be carrying us both out in the back of an ambulance."

"Hah!" she said, and surged forward.

"Look out!" Damian bellowed at her from behind. He stopped for a minute to inspect the bottom of his shoes. "There're all sorts of surprises lying in wait for us all over the ground."

"I think you've just got to plunge in, Damian," Alana said and, with that, she made a sudden wild dash toward the barn doors.

"Come on, come on," she waved cheerily to Damian, who still stood looking about him with great uncertainty.

"Don't rush me. Don't rush me," he said, "it's just dumb luck that you made it there in one fragrant piece."

He picked his way very nimbly to the door, at times balancing himself on his tiptoes with arms flung wide for added balance. Alana's peals of laughter brought a cluster of people to the door. By the time Damian had almost managed to make it to where she stood, most of the steelband players had stopped playing, and were watching the spectacle from the door. A loud round of cheering broke out as he reached a slab of clean concrete. One of the men came forward to slap Damian on the shoulder. "Man, ah neva' seen something like that before."

Damian laughed good-naturedly. To Alana he said, "Wait til I get you alone, missy."

Alana gave him a saucy wink. "Don't worry, you won't."

Introductions were made all around. The players were a very friendly group and, after a round of good-natured jokes, all directed at Damian, a few of the men helped place some folding chairs in front of the band for their guests. The leader of the steelband said, "Sit back an' relax, people. This is music done the Trinidadian way."

And the music which Alana had heard from the car, several blocks away, began again. They played song after song, going from a rousing Trinidadian socca to a soft and weepy love ballad. They even played classical numbers by Bach and Beethoven. Alana listened in speechless wonder to the music, to the clear and sweet melody of it all. It was indescribable. Growing up in Guyana, she had, of course, heard steelband music before, but not like this, not like this.

At some point during a particularly good rendition of Michael Jackson's "The Girl is Mine," Damian leaned over to whisper in her ear. "They *are* the best damn musicians in the world."

Alana nodded and squeezed his hand. At some time during the whole thing, their hands had reached out unconsciously, and were now tightly clasped. To Alana it seemed right, somehow, to be holding his hand and experiencing the glorious music with him. Suddenly, she was no longer in a shabby barn, seated on a hard metal chair and surrounded by countless farm and do-

mestic animals: she was wherever it was the music took
her.

After about forty-five minutes, there was a break of
ten minutes for Trinidadian-style cheese sandwiches
and long glasses of mango lemonade filled to the brim
with crushed ice. The men milled about, laughing and
talking. Alana sipped from her glass and chatted happily with the taxi driver. This was truly the most wonderful experience she had ever had.

Damian disappeared for a bit, and then reappeared
with the bandleader at his side. Alana gave them a
cheery little wave, and they came over to rejoin the
semicircle of musicians that had somehow gathered
around her.

Damian took up a proprietorial position behind her
chair. He rested his hands on her shoulders as though
he were protecting her. The bandleader gave the surrounding men a little signal with his hands.

Damian continued to stand behind her even after the
crowd had dispersed. After they had gone, he bent close
to her ear and whispered, "So . . . what stories have you
been entertaining the band with, my dear?"

Alana glanced up at him, uncertain of his mood. She
didn't like the tight way in which he had said the words
"my dear." He had seemed perfectly happy just seconds
before, too. He was such a moody creature, not at all
blessed with the even temperament that she had.

"I was telling them about Hanta Banta."

A slight furrow ran across Damian's forehead. "A
place in Guyana?"

She shook her head. "Far from it. In some West Indian islands they call it 'ketchin' the spirit.' She spoke
using the patois vernacular, and a little smile twitched
at the corners of Damian's mouth.

Alana wrinkled her nose at him. "In Guyana we just call it Hanta Banta. When you catch Hanta Banta you're supposed to literally dance and spin on your head while foaming at the mouth. According to those who have witnessed it, it's an extremely frightening sight. It's said to happen whenever people are possessed by tormented spirits of the dead. There's . . ."

She paused to give him a quick look. He had moved to sit beside her and was now listening with great interest. The steelband players were almost completely reassembled, and some were beginning to pick out little snatches of song on their pans.

"I'd better tell you the rest later," Alana whispered to him.

He glanced at his watch. "There probably isn't going to be a later. After the next session you're going to have to head back to the hotel to collect your luggage. You can't leave me with half a story."

Alana smiled at him. "I guess you'll just have to come to Guyana if you want to hear the rest."

Damian raised his eyebrows. "And what would your husband have to say about that?"

Their eyes met for a second. "All right, all right, I'll tell you the rest. At least all that I know. There's this place in Guyana called Papaya, you see. And, according to legend, back in either the eighteenth or nineteenth century, thousands of runaway slaves were horribly butchered there. So the story is that, whenever conga drums are played at Papaya, anyone susceptible to the tormented spirits that roam there catches Hanta Banta, goes into a trance, and dances on their heads."

"And you believe this?"

Alana shrugged. "I've never seen it happen myself, but who's to say that it's not true?"

He laughed. "And you call yourself a scientist. How did you come to be talking about that, anyway?"

"I don't know, really, we just kind of drifted into it, I guess. You know. . . ." She turned to look at him again. "If you really want an in-depth understanding of the history, legends, and folklore of the African peoples of the world, you should read some of the books written by D.C. Lynch. He's one of the foremost authorities on the subject."

Damian gave a noncommittal grunt.

Alana gave him a little tap on the arm. "He's brilliant. Really. I just love his work. When I was at Oxford I used to . . ."

The steelband chose just that exact moment to resume playing, and the remainder of her words were drowned out by the music.

For the next hour they listened to the splendid music. When, finally, Damian glanced at his watch and said, "I think we'd better go," Alana groaned and begged, "Let's listen for just a while longer." She couldn't tell him that there was a very good chance that she might never get the opportunity to do something quite like this again.

He gave her a tolerant smile and said, "Ten minutes. I don't want you to miss your flight."

Alana knew that she should have been pleased by his concern, but instead she felt strangely deflated. He was in such a hurry to get rid of her. So what if she missed her flight? Shouldn't he be pleased about that?

At about twelve twenty-five, they said their good-byes. Alana shook hands with everyone in the band.

"I've never had such a good time," she told them all, smiling. "You should tour the Caribbean, Guyana included. I'd love the chance to hear you again."

The bandleader thanked her and promised that they would be doing a tour very soon. "We're thinking of calling ourselves the Melody Makers."

"Great name," Damian said.

Alana nodded in agreement. "Perfect name."

The bandleader walked them to the door, and shook hands with them both.

"Thanks, again," Damian said.

"You and your wife must come back again," the bandleader said, smiling. "Maybe at carnival time?"

Damian looked down at Alana, and she felt the rush of blood to her face. She could tell that he was laughing inside. But "We'd love to come back," was all he said.

The taxi driver pulled the car up close to the front door and they climbed in. As they drove off, the sounds of music drifted after them. Alana strained to listen until there was nothing more. She didn't feel much like talking at all, and Damian was strangely quiet too. It was a few minutes before she realized that the driver was peering at them anxiously in the rearview mirror. She gave him a little smile, which seemed to encourage him.

"All you had a nice time?" he asked.

Alana tried to answer, but couldn't. Damian replied in a flat voice, "It was great."

The driver nodded. "I know all you have to return to de hotel soon. . . ."

Damian glanced at his watch. "Yes. We . . . ah, we . . . have to be at the airport no later than two."

The driver grinned. "Two o'clock? Man, we have plenty of time. Plenty of time. I'll take you for a quick spin down Maracas way. Beautiful countryside there. It's de best damn countryside in the whole world, you hear? The best damn countryside."

"How long will it take us to go up there and back?" Damian asked.

The taxi driver pursed his lips. "No more than half an hour."

Damian looked at Alana. "Do you want to chance it?"

Alana gave her watch a quick look. There was still a whole hour and a half to go, and it would only take half an hour to get to this Maracas place and back. And she had never done anything really senseless in her entire life, so she was entitled to this one bit of folly. What could it hurt, after all? She would never see Damian again after this. For many reasons, the chances of them ever meeting again were slim to none.

Her eyes were big and soft when she looked back up at him. For some reason, his face held that strange kindness again. For a minute, she wondered if he had guessed that she was having a difficult time letting go of him. She wanted to tell him that he had taken some strange and powerful hold on her. That she had never felt this way before, and didn't understand why it had happened. But she knew that he would not understand. At best, he might think that she was a little crazy. And maybe she was.

She blinked a couple of times, then said bravely, "All right. Let's go. We still have a little time to spare."

Three

The road to Maracas was all hill and valley. Alana cranked down the window on her side so that the refreshing breeze could whip through the car. The countryside was even more gorgeous than the taxi driver had said. It was peppered by lush greens, splashes of sudden purple, and surprising reds. There were even parts of the surrounding landscape which appeared to be actually golden. The squawks of tiny wild parakeets in the distance caused Alana to lean out the window. Her eyes glowed with the wonderment of a child.

"Have you ever seen anything quite so . . . so . . ." She was at a loss for words.

". . . Indescribable." Damian finished her sentence for her without thinking.

Alana nodded at him. "I never knew . . ." she said. "I never knew . . . This should be on a postcard somewhere . . ."

Damian nodded and unconsciously stroked the long tendrils of hair back from her face. Alana turned her head to look at him and felt a peculiar jolt go through her. She turned away quickly. The minutes were steadily ticking away. She mustn't become even more attached to him than she already was. She felt his hand stroke her face again, and closed her eyes. If she lived to be one hundred years old, she would always remember

this. The green countryside, the pungent fragrance of
flowers, the warm sunshine, and Damian.

It was during this moment, with her eyes closed, that
there was a loud explosion from one side of the car.
Alana was thrown backward against Damian, and the
car lurched crazily from left to right before coming to
a shuddering halt on the dirt embankment running the
length of the road. Alana's heart pounded hard and
heavy in her chest. What was happening? Had they been
shot? Were they being ambushed? A horrible thought
suddenly occurred to her. Were Damian and the taxi
driver part of some terrible plot to kidnap her? Was
that why they were now on this very deserted country
road in the middle of practically nowhere?

"Take your hands off me." She was almost wild with
panic as Damian attempted to help her back into an
upright position.

"Take it easy. Take it easy," he said. "We've had a
blowout."

Alana looked around quickly. She had expected to
see a pack of masked men armed with semiautomatic
weapons around the car. But there was only a solitary
brown cow grazing at the side of the road. And the road
wasn't deserted at all, something which she hadn't noticed during the peak of her fright. There were a couple
of small houses dotting the landscape. She could even
see clotheslines with laundry flapping in the breeze.
Her heartbeat began to steady with every fresh breath.
The taxi driver was already outside inspecting the tire.
Damian pushed open the door on his side and got out.

"Stay here," he said, "I'm going to give him a hand."

Within a few minutes he was back.

"The spare tire's flat. So he's going to take it up to
that house." He nodded in the direction of the closest

house. "He said he knows somebody up there who can patch it up."

Alana looked at her watch, and Damian nodded.

"Don't worry. It won't take very long. There's a little stream down the hill if you want to take a look while we wait. Or, if you rather, we can go up to the house with him."

Alana opened the door and got out. "Let's go down to the stream."

They walked across the road and down the gently sloping green in silence. At the lip of the water, Damian bent to collect a handful of tiny round stones. He shook them back and forth in his hand for a moment. There was a slight frown between his eyes as he squinted into the sun. He was the first to break the silence.

"So . . . this has been quite a tour, hasn't it?"

"Yes. It's definitely the best time I've ever had. And much better than anything we could've done on our own." She shielded her eyes against the sun, and looked up at him. She still felt a bit silly about her panicky behavior back in the car. "We'll have to pay the driver well."

Damian nodded. "I'll take care of it."

"Do you know, we don't even know his name. He really should be recommended to the tourist board."

She knew that she was rambling a bit, but she didn't care. She needed to talk about ordinary things. She didn't want to start thinking about Damian, and never seeing him again.

Damian skipped a stone across the surface of the water so that it jumped and bounced its way almost to the other bank.

He offered her a stone. "See if you can beat that."

Alana wrinkled her nose at him. "No problem at all. My br—I used to do this all the time as a child."

She launched her stone with a graceful arch of her

arm and watched in disbelief as it landed with a loud plunk somewhere near the mid-point of the stream and rapidly sank to the riverbed.

Damian laughed loudly.

"That's just about the worst performance I've ever seen."

Alana made a wild snatch at his hand. "Let me have another one. That was just my warm-up throw."

Damian evaded her and, instead, scooped up a handful of water and flung it at her. What ensued thereafter was a madcap water fight which left both participants half drenched.

Damian finally begged off. "Truce. Truce," he said, holding up his arms in surrender.

Alana wasn't ready to stop yet. "Are you sorry?" she asked.

Damian grinned at her. "Very sorry."

"Do you apologize for your earlier comments?"

"Yes. Yes. You win. You're the best."

"OK, then." She gave him a big smile and watched an unreadable expression flicker for a moment in his eyes.

"Come here," he said.

Alana was unsure of his intention, so she approached him slowly. Was he going to douse her with water again? She was ready to sprint away from him if he tried any such thing.

When she was close enough, Damian pulled out a large white handkerchief. And, slowly, like a sculptor working on a fragile piece, he dried the tiny droplets of water from Alana's face. She stood perfectly still as he stroked. She could feel the blood pulsing at the different pressure points in her body, and it was necessary to take slow deep breaths to still the violent pounding of her heart. She knew that he was going to kiss her, and more than that, she wanted him to. Maybe she had wanted him to from the start. From the very first moment. Maybe she had wanted to feel both of his hands on her face, caressing, as they were doing now.

Maybe in some previous life she had experienced all this with him. Maybe that was the reason it all seemed so familiar. God, maybe she really was crazy.

She took a little breath of air as his head blocked out the sun. He really was going to kiss her. She tilted her head up. Her lips were literally tingling in anticipation. His fingers slid into her hair to cradle the base of her skull. The rough pads of each thumb stroked across her cheekbones in a way that did peculiar things to her stomach. She closed her eyes and waited. It was a full minute before she realized that the loud honking noise coming from the road was probably due to their taxi driver's frantic attempts to locate his two passengers. She forced her eyes back open and, for a quick moment, debated the wisdom of asking him to kiss her anyway and to ignore the driver honking away relentlessly on the road.

But it would seem that he had already lost interest in it. He was actually looking at his watch. Alana gritted her teeth.

"We'd . . . we'd better go back up."

Damian ran his hands down the sides of her face, down her shoulders and her arms, then all the way to the tips of her fingers. There was a pleased expression on his face, and Alana gave him a little smile. He pinched the tip of her nose, then linked his fingers with hers. "Let's go up. I don't want you to miss your flight."

They walked slowly back up the hill. Alana kept her head bowed. This was it. For the rest of her life, never, never would she see him again. The enormity of it brought the prickle of tears to the back of her eyes. Why had they both been on the same flight over from Britain? Why couldn't the flight have been as uneventful as all the other flights which she had taken before? Why? Why . . . ? Her brain was churning with a mixture of confusion and despair.

Alana barely noticed the expression of relief on the driver's face as his two passengers reappeared on the road. Damian whispered in her ear, "He probably thought we'd run off and left him."

Alana managed a half-hearted chuckle, but not much else.

At the car, the taxi driver and Damian exchanged a humorous comment about their disheveled state— something about honeymooners and Christmastime— Alana didn't really listen. The spare was now on the car, and Damian gave it a solid tap with the toe of his shoe before helping Alana into the backseat. He climbed in after her and closed the door.

"We're gonna have to cut short the rest of the trip and head back to the hotel. Got a plane to catch at two."

The taxi driver nodded. "All you need much more time than a couple of hours if you want to really see Trinidad. Some of de places I could take you to, you wouldn't believe. And don't start me talking about Tobago. Tobago is de best damn little island in de wo'ld, you hear? De best damn little island."

All the way back, Alana listened to the driver's bright chatter. She forced herself to listen and to participate in the discussion, which ranged from cricket to politics in the Caribbean. Alana noticed that Damian nodded, more than anything else, and she finally decided that he probably knew very little about the topics of discussion and had, therefore, wisely decided to remain silent.

The trip back was over in a remarkably quick time. Alana couldn't believe it, as they pulled to a stop in front of the hotel. The driver swooped agilely into a space at the curb and sprang out. It took less than five minutes for thank-you's to be said and the fare to be paid. The business card which Alana put safely into her pocketbook said simply: "Phil's Taxi Service. The Best Tours in Trinidad & Tobago."

Alana shook Phil's hand warmly and told him that she would remember the trip for the rest of her life. Damian shook hands, too, and echoed Alana's sentiment. He gave Phil two hundred U.S. dollars for the tour and an additional hundred as a tip.

The taxi driver seemed shocked, and he tried to give some of the money back. "It's too much," he said. "I don't want de tourist board to think I'm taking advantage."

Damian grinned. "If they give you a hard time about it, let them know that you earned every penny."

"All right." Phil gave Damian another hearty handshake. "You and your wife must come back to T&T again. And ask for Phil next time. Listen . . . all you want a lift to the airport? It's no problem."

But this time Damian turned him down. He slapped him on the shoulder and assured him that they had already booked a trip on the airport shuttle. Phil took defeat well and wished them a safe flight home.

In the elevator, going up, Alana said, "I could've taken him to the airport."

Damian smiled. "And ruin his impression of our marital bliss? Never."

Alana looked at the little digital panel above the door and blinked furiously. She promised herself that she would remember everything, including the little red numbers above the elevator door which indicated the floor.

"I'll just get my things and be out of your hair."

"I'm coming with you."

The little ping the door made as it slid open blotted out his words, and Alana wasn't sure she had heard him correctly.

"Wh . . . what?"

"I said that I'm coming with you to the airport." He shrugged. "It's the least I can do. That bag you have in there is quite heavy."

She gave him a little uncertain look. "Well . . . if you're sure it's no trouble."

Damian opened the door to the suite and ushered her inside. "Would you like a bite to eat before we go?"

Alana gave her watch a quick look. "Not enough time. Besides, the flight to Guyana's very short. I'll get something to eat later."

Damian nodded. "Well, you'd better get your bags, then. I'll wait out here unless you think you'll need help bringing them out."

Alana assured him that she could manage very nicely on her own and wouldn't need any help at all. She was in and out of the bedroom in less than ten minutes. Her main bag was already packed, and it only took a few minutes to collect together the few toiletries she had left on the vanity in the bathroom. She checked under the bed for anything that might have fallen out of sight, then zipped everything closed.

Damian was standing at the bank of windows in the sitting room when she returned. He seemed like such a solitary figure, standing there all alone, and Alana observed him for a moment in silence. She hadn't noticed it before, but there was something lonely about him. For the thousandth time, she wished she hadn't told him that she was married. Would he understand if she told him now, and explained why she had felt it necessary to fabricate such a story? Maybe she had made some small sound, or maybe he just sensed her presence, for he turned at that moment.

Their eyes met, and a little shiver went through her. "Ready to go?"

"Yes." Her voice croaked in the most unattractive way. And she felt sure that a smile flickered across his face.

He walked over and stood looking down at her for what felt like minutes. She looked deeply into the black, inky depths of his eyes, and the words "maybe he'll kiss me now" beat an insistent tattoo in her brain. Her heart leapt as he leaned toward her. The pounding in her chest was so intense that it actually hurt a little. He was going to . . . He was going to?

She watched in disbelief as he seemed to miss her face entirely. It was a few dazed seconds before she realized that he'd actually been reaching downward to pick up her suitcase. And he appeared to be completely unaware of what she'd been expecting him to do. She bent to grab up the remaining bags at her feet. What in the world was the matter with him? Didn't he have a heart? Didn't he have hot blood rushing through his veins? She walked briskly ahead of him to pull open the door.

At the elevator he asked, "Are you all right?"

She took a deep breath, and then released it. "Yes. I'm fine." She was being ridiculous. If he didn't want to kiss her, even though she had practically begged him to, that was entirely his choice. Maybe he didn't find her attractive. She played with that possibility all the way down to the lobby floor. She was still thinking about it as they sat side by side in the airport shuttle. Maybe he was just one of those very helpful types. A grown-up boy scout. The kind who liked to help a damsel in distress, or something like that. Why had he chosen to help *her*, then? He was making her life a living hell.

"What's that?"

Alana jumped as his bare arm brushed against the tender flesh of her elbow.

She must have spoken aloud.

"Nothing. I was just thinking.

"You said something about living in hell."

"Ah . . . yes. I was just thinking how strange it is that certain people can live in hell, and certain other people just don't even seem to care at all."

He turned in his seat to look at her. There was a worried expression on his face. "Are you feeling light-headed?"

"No. I feel fine, just fine."

"You should have had something to eat."

She gave him a big smile. "We don't always get what we should, do we?"

His brows were wrinkled, now, and Alana was glad she wasn't making any sense. Served him right if he couldn't understand a word she was saying. He had caused it, after all, by being extremely blind, and extremely stupid. What did he want her to do? How much clearer could she be?

"Lie back and close your eyes. You'll feel better. Let me open up the window. There."

A blast of air hit Alana squarely in the face as the window popped open. Her hair whipped about her head, and swatches of it hit Damian across the face.

Alana struggled with the window for a minute, then yanked it closed. She turned a very tousled head in Damian's direction.

"Why did you do that?"

He swept some of the hair off her face. "Feeling better, I see. Totally coherent again."

Alana brushed her hair back with her fingers. "I was not incoherent. You just didn't understand me."

The shuttle pulled to a stop outside the terminal. Damian gave her hair another brush with his fingers.

"Would you like to borrow my comb?"

Alana pulled out her compact and took a quick look at her hair. "Seems like whenever I turn up at this airport, my hair's a mess." She wound the long strands into a thick braid and said, "This will have to do."

Damian carried her suitcase up to the check-in, then stood waiting. The line this time was much more orderly. She was told that the flight to Guyana would be leaving in exactly one hour. Boarding would begin in twenty-five minutes. After going through all the formalities of check-in, she walked back over to where Damian stood.

"Well," she said, "this is good-bye, I guess."

Damian took her by the elbow and walked her away from the crowd. "I think you should have something to eat."

Right at that moment, Alana's stomach cringed at the thought of food. She was beginning to feel very numb inside. Everything was beginning to feel very unreal. It was as though she were watching a movie, as though she wasn't really there and a part of it all.

"I don't feel . . . very hungry somehow."

"Something sweet then. A box of chocolates to nibble on the plane in case you start feeling hungry then?"

"All right," she agreed grudgingly, knowing she didn't really want chocolates, either.

The duty-free shop was almost empty, and she followed him half-heartedly to the shelf where all the nicely wrapped boxes were stacked.

"How about this one?"

He pointed to a bright package of pink and white caramel clusters.

"OK." This was where she had met him in Britain; now this was where she was saying good-bye.

He pulled the box from the shelf and presented it to

her with a flourish. "I'm sure your husband won't mind such a gift . . . between friends?"

Alana blinked up at him. She was barely managing to keep the tears from forming great big pools in her eyes. She couldn't stand it. She had to go, and now, before she broke down entirely. Maybe she should tell him now that she wasn't really married, since she wasn't ever going to see him again. He deserved the truth.

"Damian . . . I . . . there's . . ."

He stood looking at her with that smile in his eyes that was now so familiar.

She couldn't do it. She couldn't ruin this . . . not now.

"I . . . I think they just announced my flight. I have to go."

She watched the Adam's apple in his throat move up, then down again. He pulled her close, and his arms went around her in a tight hug.

"Take care of yourself, Alana Britton. Your husband is a very lucky man."

He gave her a quick, hard kiss on the lips. It was almost too quick for her to know that it had happened. At the door to the duty-free shop, he hugged her again. Then he was gone, walking briskly away, melting into the crowd, not looking back even once.

Four

When the announcement came for her flight, Alana boarded with blurry eyes. She tried to focus on the fact that she was happy to be going home. In less than an hour, she would see Harry again. She wouldn't think about Damian Collins at all. She would just squeeze him out of her mind as easily as he had shut her out of his. It was silly to be sad. He was just a stranger she had met on a plane, just a chance encounter. He had been kind to her, and because of that, she was grateful. The soreness at the back of her throat was not due to the fact that she had been fighting back tears all day—it was because she was a bit run-down after all the confusion of the past two days. She peered out the window, and forced herself to think of home, of everyone there who loved her, of seeing Guyana again after five whole years.

The trip over from Trinidad was very short and, before long, they were circling Timehri airport, then making the final approach for landing. Alana buckled herself in and realized with a happy feeling that the numbness she had felt in Trinidad and Tobago was beginning to fade. Her heart beat with thick heavy thumps in her chest. It would be very soon now. Harry would be there waiting. Everything would be all right.

* * *

Alana showed her official pass at the gate, then proceeded to the VIP lounge. It was practically empty when she got there. She broke into a run. Harry was there. She could see him clearly through the glass.

He met her halfway across the floor, sweeping her off her feet and spinning her around. There were tears in her eyes, and a glint of a similar emotion in his. They hugged each other for a few more seconds, then he placed her away from himself and looked at her with critical eyes.

"You've lost weight, Lani. What have you been doing to yourself?"

Her eyes sparkled up at him. Her beautiful brother. She loved him more than anyone else in the world.

"You weren't there to make me overeat."

He threw a protective arm about her shoulders and hugged her close. "I'm here now, and we'll never be separated again."

"Promise?" she asked, her eyes shining with hidden mischief, just like when they'd been children.

He squeezed her again. "Promise."

Alana slid into the black Rolls Royce that stood at the curb. The seats were a fawn color, soft and comfortable. She rolled down the window and kicked off her shoes. Night was beginning to fall, and the feeling of home swept over her. The frogs had already begun their nightly chorus, and the breeze stirred the treetops, sending a whisper-soft song echoing through the night. She turned to her brother, and he smiled at her.

"It's so good to be home. It's still a surprise that I'm here, isn't it? Mom and Dad still don't know?"

Harry nodded. "I haven't told them, though I can't

say I understand why you've wanted to keep them in the dark about this."

Alana glanced at her brother, her start of surprise hidden. He'd always understood and supported her, yet she was certain that there had been a slight note of censure in his voice.

"You know what would've happened if I'd arrived officially. I wanted to avoid my return being splashed all over the newspaper. Remember what happened last year with you."

He linked his fingers with hers and gave her a considering look. "I know it's hard being the daughter of the Prime Minister. It gets in the way of a lot of things."

Alana smiled at him. He did understand. She was on the verge of telling him about Damian Collins and the fact that she had found it necessary to let him believe that she was married but, for some reason, she discovered that she didn't want to discuss that yet. Damian Collins had made her uncomfortable, had made her wonder what her life might have been like if she had been free of the responsibilities that came with being the daughter of a high official.

The Soesdyke Highway, along which they were now headed, was a long stretch of winding two-laned road, cut through miles of densely forested land. But there was nothing sinister about the thick green foliage which bordered either side of the highway. The Soesdyke linked the bauxite mining town of Linden to the capital city, Georgetown. It was a serene sixty-five miles, and it had always been one of Alana's favorite places. The majesty of the towering trees which cloaked the road in a shroud of silence could, just as suddenly, be disturbed by the flutter of parakeets or the slow, unhurried crawl of a one-toed sloth. The sandy coral white banks, which

sloped away from the road, were a favorite picnic spot
for many people, especially at Easter. It was Alana's
fondest dream one day to be able to stop there and
soak in the delicate scenery without the presence of a
bodyguard. But maybe it was an unattainable dream,
because she couldn't see it coming true at all, any time
soon.

Somewhere on the edge of Linden, Harry shook her,
and Alana realized that they were nearly home. They
had crested the last hill, and the lights of the mining
town could be seen spread out for miles. The feeling
of nostalgia that gripped Alana was so great that, for a
minute, she couldn't speak. Nowhere else on earth
could inspire this feeling of belonging—this deep sense
of home.

A few minutes later, they were at the gated estate in
Watooka. As the car pulled up in the circular driveway,
a uniformed guard rushed to open the door. Another
two stood at rigid attention as Alana and her brother
climbed from the car. Harry grinned down at her from
his formidable height.

"You're here. Do you remember the place?"

She poked him in the side just as the double lacquered front doors sprang open, and she recognized
her mother's secretary. She was a tall, dark woman in
her mid fifties. She was practically a member of the
family now. She had been with them since Alana and
Harry were children.

Miss Lewis's eyes fell on Harry, then widened in shock
as she realized that the young woman standing next to
him was Alana. She rushed forward, her hands out-
stretched.

"Lani, my dear. You're home. You didn't let us know
you were coming. Your parents . . ." Alana was envel-

oped in her motherly embrace, then hustled into the house with the secretary clucking over her like a startled hen.

Her mother was in the first sitting room, dictating a letter, as they swept in. She was as elegant as ever, dressed in a svelte cream-and-lace affair that gave her the polished air of sophistication expected of the wife of the Prime Minister. She turned to see what the commotion was about, and dropped the small recorder in her hand when she saw her daughter. Alana sped into her mother's arms, and was at once admonished and kissed. It took several minutes to explain to her mother why she had not let them know that she would be home for Christmas, but Harry soothed the situation in his expert and concise fashion.

Much later, after a phone call to her father, who was still in Georgetown, Alana retired to her suite of rooms on the third floor of the house. It was a complete apartment in itself, with its own sitting and dining rooms. Her clothes had been unpacked and placed on padded hangers in a walk-in closet that was bigger than most people's bedrooms. There was nothing for her to do, and Alana felt slightly at a loss. She had grown quite accustomed, in the last five years, to taking care of herself, and wished her mother would understand that there was no need for anyone to fetch and carry for her as though she were an invalid.

She took a leisurely bath, and found herself thinking back on the events of the last twenty-four hours. Damian Collins's face kept looming up before her, no matter how hard she tried to concentrate and shut thoughts of him out.

Finally, in frustration, she stepped from the tub and towelled dry in short, brisk strokes. She dressed in a white printed silk jumpsuit, and was in the process of taming her thick mane of hair when Harry appeared. He was dressed for bed, and Alana's eyebrows rose in question.

"Aren't you going down for dinner?"

"No. I have to work on my briefs for tomorrow's session in court." He sprawled in a wicker chair and watched her as she scraped her hair back severely from her face.

"Lani, you do remember we both have to attend the President's Ball on Old Year's Night?"

Alana turned from the mirror. "Can't you stand in for me? I really don't feel up to going to such a big event."

Harry gave her a rueful smile. "I tried to convince Dad that you should have a bit of a rest." He lifted his shoulders in a slight shrug. "But you know how he feels about duty."

Alana finished securing her hair. "Well, at least I had a five-year break from it all." Her eyes lit up with a sudden spark of fun. "Maybe I should do another doctorate, this time in Alaska."

Harry reached out and enveloped her in a brotherly hug. "Come on, it won't be so bad. We'll be together."

Alana nodded. He was right, there were much worse things. Besides, it was the season of goodwill, and Christmas had always been a happy time for the Brittons. The house would be filled with pine trees in every room, dripping gorgeous baubles of shimmering red, blue, and gold. Favorite Christmas hymns would fill the air, and a softer mood would settle over the family. And on Christmas Eve, as evening fell, everyone would gather by the resplendent Christmas tree in the main sitting room, turn off all the lights, and sing lustily as Harry strummed out song after song on his box guitar. And they would be like any other family. No talk of politics, just laughter and good old-fashioned fun. The pungent aroma of rum and wine from the thick black cakes, and the sharp sweet smell of casareep, which gave the traditional Christmas dish of pepperpot its distinctive flavor, would help to keep everyone in high spirits.

Alana smiled and squeezed Harry's hand. Yes, Christmas would be good. The parties didn't really matter.

Five

Christmas Eve that year found them seated as they had been in the past: Harry and Alana on the floor before the tree, their parents side by side on the settee. It was especially poignant for them all, not just because it was the season of joy. It was the first Christmas in five years that they could all spend together.

Miss Lewis, who always stayed with them until Christmas Day, hustled in now from the kitchen. She carried huge slabs of crusty mango pie. Harry waylaid her before she could set the tray down, grabbing the largest piece for himself. She slapped his hand with an expression of mock severity on her face. Harry grinned cheerfully, completely unruffled. He ladled thick helpings of sweet cream onto his slice, and devoured it with obvious enjoyment. Then he sidled over to Alana, and attempted to snatch her piece when she wasn't looking. What ensued next was the first food fight they had had in years. Laughing, Mrs. Britton broke them apart, even as Harry snarled playfully at Alana and she threatened him with a puny fist. Alana looked into her mother's eyes, and saw the reflection of heartfelt joy. Mr. Britton stood and wrapped an arm around his wife, and Alana thought that he looked suspiciously misty himself. With echoes of "Merry Christmas" all around, a feeling of deep contentment stole over her. It was good to be home. She had pushed all thoughts of Damian Collins out of her mind. Even though his face popped into her head at the most inconvenient times, she was determined not to let that dampen her Christmas spirits. She would never see the man again, and she had to accept that.

Later, after everyone had retired to bed, Alana stood by one of the huge meshed windows at the back of the house and looked out at the Demerara River. In the darkness, it shimmered like a tight band of silk, silent and unfathomable. The black waters were deceptively calm, giving no indication of the dangerous currents which lurked just beneath the surface. In some parts, the river was infested by piranha but, despite this, Alana had always found something soothing about the huge body of water. It was like a faithful friend, always there, always the same. There was something comforting in its constancy. She'd always felt that if all the world changed, the Demerara would remain just as it had always been.

She was so deep in thought that she failed to hear the soft footfalls behind her until she was grabbed from behind. She barely managed to suppress a startled shriek as she heard her brother's voice.

"Harry! You almost scared me half to death."

He stood beside her, looking in the direction of the river. "Remember how we used to fish back there?"

Alana nodded, her eyes huge in the darkness. "And when Mom found out, we couldn't sit down for a week."

Harry chuckled. "It was fun though, wasn't it? Worth the risk."

Alana gave him a sideways glance. "You were always getting me into trouble."

"Is that so? Remember the time you tied the ambassador of Britain's son to the guava tree, and told him that the Masacurra man was coming to get him at midnight? You almost caused an international incident."

Alana giggled. "He was a horrible little brat. I could have done much worse."

"Or how about when you poured glue into that maid's shoe . . . what was her name again?"

"Susan," Alana said, a trace of regret in her voice. "We were terrible children."

Harry hugged her. "Ah, but look how well we've turned out." He turned her to face him, his eyes searching hers. Alana tried to duck her head, because there was no hiding from Harry. Where she was concerned, he was as sharp as a blade.

"Are you going to tell me what's wrong?"

She looked at him for a second, and considered whether or not she should unburden herself to him.

"It's . . ."

"Come on, Lani," Harry shook her. "Nothing could be that bad."

"I'm tired of being trapped by all this. I know many people probably envy us, but wouldn't it be great to be free? Free to do anything at all you wanted to do? No bodyguards, no state functions, just . . ."

"Ah hah," he said, as though he had finally gotten to the root of things. "It's a man."

Alana stuttered. "Don't be ridiculous. I'm talking about . . ."

Harry nodded in an irritatingly knowledgeable way. "I know what you're talking about. What's his name?"

"Damian." Alana muttered, infuriated with herself for being so weak. She had promised herself that she would not think of him again.

Harry rolled the name around his tongue. "I don't like it. He sounds like a Pacoo to me."

Alana snickered. Every Guyanese understood what that meant. A Pacoo was a particularly ugly and stupid fish, with a big head and huge bulging eyes. It was not a flattering description.

"He said the same about you. Said your name lacked character, or something like that."

Harry's eyes widened in amusement. "I think I'd like to meet this man," he folded his fist. "He'd soon find out how much character I lacked."

Alana held his arm. "Can you find him for me?"

"In Britain?"

"Or Trinidad. He seems to travel a lot."

A worried frown crept over Harry's face and Alana felt her heart sink. Harry was far too protective of her. He wouldn't help.

"What does he do?"

Alana shrugged, already knowing what was coming next. "I'm not sure. I know he's American. I mean, he sounds more American . . . than British. He could be Canadian, too, I guess. And I suppose it's possible that he might even be a . . . a fortune hunter."

"You mean gigolo?"

"Ok, that then." Alana responded a little huffily.

"No, I can't help." His answer held a note of finality, and was what she'd expected him to say. It had been a crazy idea to ask him, a ridiculous impulse.

"I'm not going to let some creep take advantage of you. He probably met you on the plane, I suppose?" When she nodded, he continued. "Lani, I keep telling you that you have to be more aware. I'm sure he knew who you were from the start. A Prime Minister's daughter is a good catch."

In her mind, Alana rushed back over the events as they had unfolded in Trinidad. Could that have been the reason why he had been so kind and helpful? Had he known who she was, all along? Had he been mapping out some horrible and sordid scheme for scandal? Had he been secretly amused when she had told him that she was married?

"But . . . he was very nice . . . I really don't think he knew . . ."

Harry gripped her shoulders. "You're a scientist, Lani, trained to be analytical. Think about it. Really think about it, then tell me if what I'm saying doesn't make sense. He probably sized you up and decided that a gentle approach would work best with you. I wouldn't be a bit surprised to find that he's followed you to Guyana. You're a prize, my sweet innocent, and men like Damian what's-his-face are like bloodhounds when it comes to money." He gave a cynical little laugh. "Believe me, I won't have to find him. If I'm right, he'll find you."

Alana sighed. She felt decidedly sorry for herself. "But, he thought . . . he really believed that I was married. That my name was Britton by marriage. If he knew who I was, he wouldn't have believed that."

"What makes you so sure he did believe it?"

Alana went to bed feeling even more poorly than before the heart-to-heart talk with her brother. Life just wasn't fair. She didn't know who to trust anymore. Somebody was always out for something. She never knew whether people liked her for herself, or because she was the P.M.'s daughter. It bothered her intensely, and she couldn't understand why Harry seemed totally unaffected by the entire situation of their birth.

The next few days passed in a whirl of activity. They journeyed amidst much fanfare to the capital city of Georgetown, where there were the obligatory visits to make to the families of other senior officials, and the usual itinerary of holiday cocktail parties, which Alana detested. By the time Old Year's Night arrived, Alana had had her fill of social events, and was on the verge of telling Harry that she would not be able to attend the President's Ball with him.

She stood in her bedroom, and gave herself a critical once-over in the mirror. Her hair fell in thick, gleaming curls. Her complexion, already flawless, was made even more so by the skillful application of makeup. Her eyebrows had been tamed into a smooth arch, and across her lips was the barest hint of amber. She had chosen a slinky saffron dress which was deceptively conservative in the front, then scooped low in the back to reveal creamy sable skin. She gave her lips a final blot with a napkin, then turned the lights out. On the way down, she received quite a few surreptitious stares from her father's aides, and wondered for the hundredth time at the wisdom of wearing such a dress to a party where she would, without encouragement, be the target of unwanted advances from ambitious young men.

Harry was already standing by the car, and he turned to greet her, his lips pursed in an exaggerated wolf whistle. She smiled cheekily at him. He looked rather splendid himself, dressed in a silky, dark green shirt and tapered black slacks. Even at his most casual, he exuded a sensuality and charisma that attracted women in droves. He was a handsome devil, by anyone's standards.

The car took them across town then down the long stretch of Vlisengen Road. The Residence, the official home of the President of Guyana, was ablaze with light, and after passing through the guarded entrance, the car came to a halt at the lip of the front stairs. There were already many people milling about the lawns, and Alana shot Harry a quick look. He seemed completely relaxed, a stark contrast to the turmoil she was feeling. Instead of looking forward to the evening ahead, she saw it as an ordeal to be suffered through.

Harry opened the door and helped her out. He gave her chin a quick pinch, then whispered, "Let's mingle. And don't forget to say hello to the President before we leave tonight."

They were at once engulfed in a throng of people, and Alana found herself cornered by a couple of matrons who were determined to explain to her why they thought the Third World was in the kind of economic trouble it was in. Alana listened politely while managing to cast an eye about for Harry. The lawns were becoming more crowded now and, from where she stood, Alana could see many ambassadors and other foreign dignitaries whom she recognized.

There was a long curving bar set up at the far side of the lawn, and Alana extricated herself from the two women and walked across to get some refreshments. The tinkling sounds of steelband music lent a certain gaiety to the proceedings, and Alana squeezed into a seat to watch as people began to dance. She saw a group of men eyeing her, and she hurriedly picked up a plate and began stacking it with hors d'oeuvres. The Minister of Health wandered over with a drink in his hand and, for the next few minutes, Alana chatted to him about her studies in Britain, and what she hoped to do now that she was back in the country. He asked her to dance and, soon, Alana was caught up in the crush of people swaying to, first, calypso, then, socca music. The steelband was excellent, and Alana found that she was really beginning to enjoy herself. She danced with a Ghanaian official who was dressed in traditional garb, then with the British ambassador, who was very interested in knowing what she thought of his country.

The music paused for a moment, and Alana took that

opportunity to make her way back to the bar for a glass
of lemonade. She took a refreshing sip, and scanned
the area for a free chair. It was then that she became
aware that she was being observed. He was standing
with his back against a tall palm tree. There was a drink
in his hand, but it was clear that he hadn't yet tasted
it. His eyes met hers in that bold way, and held, and
Alana felt something between excitement and fear ripple through her. For a few seconds, she wasn't sure if
the moonlight was playing tricks on her, but when he
straightened from his lazy slouch against the tree, she
knew it was really him. There had to be at least two
hundred people on the lawns now, and Alana turned
and fought her way back through the teeming mass of
people. Harry had been right about Mr. Damian Collins. He had known who she was all along. She had
hoped that somehow she might see him again, but now
that he was here, she almost felt like crying. No one
could be trusted. She was halfway across to the north
side of the lawns when she felt a tug on her arm, and
was spun into the arms of her brother. He grinned
down at her.

"Enjoying yourself?"

Alana grimaced. "I was." She went on to add, "He's
here."

Harry's eyebrows quirked upwards. "Lover boy?"

Alana nodded, then almost bit her tongue as she
spied Damian over Harry's shoulder.

"He's coming over," Alana said in a fierce whisper.

Harry swung her around, and she felt his jaw tighten.
"Not at all what I expected. He looks about ready to
pound me into the dirt."

Alana whispered again. "Maybe we'd better go." She
knew her brother. Despite his disarming charisma and
drop-dead looks, she knew that, should Damian attempt
to dance with her, Harry would pummel him senseless

with little encouragement. She could already feel the solid steel of his muscles as they tensed in readiness for a possible confrontation.

"Harry, promise me you won't start anything." She looked up at him, and she could see by the way his nostrils had begun to flare that they would be in for trouble if she didn't call a halt to it. The music stopped for a minute, and Harry clamped an arm about her waist and held her firmly at his side. Alana prayed that Damian would turn around and go back the way he'd come, but when she opened her eyes he was standing directly before them.

"Doctor Britton."

Alana's heart leapt at the sound of his voice. "Hello, Mr. Collins."

After all they had gone through together, it seemed silly to address him by his last name, but she forced herself to remember that nothing that had happened in Trinidad was real. That Damian had only been playing a part. The muscled arm about her waist flexed, and Damian's eyes flickered over it for a brief second, then returned to hers. Alana forced herself to hold his gaze. The dark eyes were as coal black as she remembered. His face was a bit thinner, almost saturnine, the way the harsh planes and angles were accentuated by the moonlight. But it was still as pullingly sensual as ever. The look he gave Harry was one of cool unconcern.

"Aren't you going to introduce us?"

A quick glance at her brother told Alana that she'd better get Harry away from Damian, and fast. He was glaring at the other man with barely concealed antagonism.

"This is Harry Britton."

Damian extended his hand, and Harry ignored it.

"How did you get in here?" he growled, not flinching as Alana gave him a none-too-gentle prod in the side.

Damian's eyes narrowed to slits, and Alana sensed that the thin veneer of sophistication that this man wore could be stripped away in a matter of seconds.

"The same way you got in, I would imagine."

The gauntlet had been tossed at Harry's feet with careless regard given to the consequences, and Alana had a sneaking suspicion that, this time, her brother might have met his match.

"Well, it was nice seeing you again," Alana said hastily, turning to drag Harry along with her. The hairs on the back of her neck were at rigid attention, and Alana knew without looking that Damian hadn't moved from where he stood. She could feel the burning intensity of his gaze, sense the dark sensuality he exuded.

"Did you see the way he looked at you?" Harry asked through gritted teeth. "It was almost as though he was undressing you right before me."

Alana gave his arm a consoling pat. "Don't get all worked up about it, Harry, it's really not worth it."

Harry gave her a grim look. "How do you suppose he got in here?"

Alana shrugged. "Maybe he was invited?"

Harry gave this possibility a few seconds of thought, then discarded it. "I doubt it. He probably swindled his way in. I've met his kind before." He gave her a reassuring squeeze. "Don't worry, I'll sort it all out."

Alana closed her eyes for a brief second. Things were beginning to get out of hand. Harry's way of sorting things out, was more often than not, nonverbal.

"Maybe we should just go home. Dad would have a fit if he heard that you'd gotten yourself mixed up in another brawl."

Harry gave her a rueful grin. "It's been years since I've been involved in anything like that."

"Two, to be exact," Alana said.

Harry maneuvered Alana into a seat, then pulled up a chair and sat directly opposite her. "I controlled myself back there, didn't I?"

"Just barely." Alana looked around, and breathed a sigh of relief that Damian was nowhere in sight.

"Listen," Harry said, leaning forward, "there's someone I have to see. Can you wait here for a few minutes? I'll ask Peters to come over. . . ."

"Go on," Alana said. "I'll be fine without Peters. I can handle Damian Collins. I'm not a child, for heaven's sake."

A quick flicker of hurt crossed Harry's face, and Alana was immediately contrite. She'd never said a harsh word to him in her life, and didn't understand why his desire to protect her should bother her now. Her hand curled over his, and she pressed a kiss to the side of his face.

"I'll be all right."

After he left, Alana scanned the crowd. Some people were standing around in small groups, others were swaying to the music in the area cleared for dancing. Damian, thankfully, was nowhere to be seen. The waiters had begun moving amongst the tables, serving the main dishes of the evening. A gentle breeze had picked up, blowing in from the Atlantic, and Alana sucked it in, enjoying the freedom of the moment. The aromas of curry and roti drifted across to her and, by the time the waiters had arrived at her table, Alana found that she had worked up a healthy appetite. She chose some of the thick spicy chicken curry, the standard roti, and a side dish of black pudding and souse. To wash everything down, she selected a large glass of ice cold Mauby. She was in the process of tearing off a piece of roti when a shadow loomed over her chair. A deep feeling of excitement ran through her as he pulled up a chair and sat down. She forced herself to scoop up some curry with the roti and place it in her mouth.

Damian watched her without comment, his eyes moving first over her face, then lingering on her mouth. He watched the undulation of the muscles in her jaw as she chewed, and Alana felt a sudden trembling overtake her.

"What is that?" He pointed a finger at the roti on her plate.

Alana swallowed with an awkward clenching movement of her throat, and her eyes and nose began to water. Damian leaned forward, and wiped her face with the flat of his palm. The feel of his skin against hers sent Alana into instant shock, and caused her to recoil from him. His mouth tightened at her reaction, and Alana rushed into a hurried discourse on the virtues of roti.

When she was through, he said, "Yes," and nodded with what appeared to be great understanding, although Alana was sure that she hadn't made much sense at all. "It does look kind of like a burrito."

"What's the other dish?" Before Alana could respond, he reached across and cut an ample slice from her roll of black pudding. He gave it a cursory inspection before popping it into his mouth and chewing with obvious enjoyment.

"I thought it was some type of sausage, but it's not, huh?"

Alana cleaned her fingers on a napkin, then forced herself to look him squarely in the eye. All this talk of food was just a lot of beating around the bush, at least on her end of things.

"Why are you here?" she asked without preamble.

"If Harry sees us together, he's likely to beat you sense-less."

Damian leaned back in his chair, his shirt pulling open at the neck to reveal a generous expanse of hair-roughened chest.

"I can take care of myself. What I'm more interested in knowing is how you come to be at this party. I had a look at the guest list, and your precious Harry is not an elected official, just a very junior barrister with"—and he paused to take a sip from her glass of Mauby before continuing, unbroken—"a penchant for street brawls. Definitely not the sort of character likely to be invited to the President's New Year's Eve bash."

Alana gaped at him for a second. Harry had been right about him. The courteous and considerate behavior in Trinidad had just been an act. How dare he criti-cize Harry, when he was probably no better than a . . . a gigolo himself. Pretending that he knew nothing of who she was. Of all the unmitigated gall, to sit there before her and lie with such ease. She would much pre-fer it if people were honest about their intentions; she respected them more. Somehow, she'd expected a little more subtlety from him. Some other pretense might have worked, but not this. Her lips curled into a hu-morless smile. "You know exactly how I got in here, and who I am."

He leaned forward, completely unperturbed by the frigid expression on her face. "Strange you don't seem happy to see me again, Alana Britton, Doctor of Chem-istry. You must remember that you practically invited me down here."

Alana pushed her plate away and prepared to stand. "I . . . did not invite you down, or imply that . . ." She paused to take a deep breath. Maybe she was at fault.

"Look . . . you were very helpful to me in Trinidad. I'm, of course, very grateful to you for that. But you know very well that there was nothing . . . nothing at all between us. I'd like to repay the favor, naturally, so just let me know what you . . ."

His face relaxed into a grin that was painfully familiar. "Lunch."

She blinked at him. "What?"

"I'll consider the favor repaid if you have lunch with me tomorrow."

She turned away, her eyes hunting the crowd for Harry. "I'm sorry; it's just not possible."

Damian ran his fingers down the front of his shirt, plucking at the buttons as though he were suddenly hot.

"I altered my schedule for you. It's the least you can do."

Alana felt a quick flash of ire. How could she have imagined that she felt anything at all for this man? The conceit of him. "I don't recall ever requesting that you rearrange your life to accommodate me. I'm a married woman, remember?" She watched him closely for his response to this. She wanted to see his eyes. She wanted to see the reaction there.

His expression was clear and unblinking. "I've thought of little else since you left Trinidad."

She pressed harder. "Doesn't marriage mean anything at all to you?"

He shrugged. "I've always found it extremely inconvenient, and in this case it's a damn nuisance."

"You mean you do this sort of thing a lot?"

He gave her a bland look. "What sort of thing?"

"Play around with married women," she said, her voice rising dangerously.

He smiled at her, and she felt like slapping him hard.

"I don't believe in adultery, myself, but desperate situations . . ." He let another shrug fill in the blanks. "I also don't believe in letting what I want slip through my fingers. When I see something that I want, I take it. And I definitely want you."

Alana felt a bead of perspiration roll down the small of her back. She stared at him, momentarily robbed of speech. He was bold, there was no question about that. From the first moment she had seen him, she had known the kind of man he was. It was there in the aggressive tilt of his chin, and in the unfathomable depths of his eyes. He was a man of intense passions. A relationship with him would be no calm affair. There would be no room for puerile emotion. It would be all or nothing, a roller coaster ride to ecstasy, and, when it was over, she would never again be the same.

She glanced down at the table, and realized that his fingers were resting lightly on her arm. It was a gentle touch, but there was nothing gentle about the way he watched her. She felt herself giving way to his silent demand, felt her will to resist him caving in under the heat of his gaze.

She closed her eyes and offered up a prayer that he not be a gigolo. The lights seemed to fade, and the background noise grow dim. The triumphant lift of his lips told her that he knew he'd won. And when he stood and pulled her into his arms, Alana wondered if she'd gone crazy. But what could it hurt to give in, if only for a few minutes.

All her life, she'd lived according to a strict code of ethics. There was right, and wrong, and nothing in between. Duty to one's country came first, family second, and everything else a dim third. But as Damian folded her to him, and she could feel the solid thud of his heart against her skin, everything that had always seemed important faded away, and all that was left was this trembling awareness that only this man could make her feel. It was as though a door had opened, and suddenly there was light where previously there had been none.

Her fingers splayed across his back and, through his shirt, his skin felt smooth and warm, and so infinitely right.

His mouth touched the side of her neck, and she couldn't suppress the shudder that rippled through her. His voice was a husky murmer, and she looked up at him. In the half light, he smiled at her. It was a smile of possession.

"I've wanted to hold you like this since the first time I saw you."

Alana turned her face away, but he shifted it back toward him. His glance touched the trembling fullness of her lips. "Alana . . ."

What he would have said was lost in an upsurge of cheering as the sound of a horn blowing heralded the passing of the old year. The lights dimmed in recognition of the birth of the new year, and in those precious moments of complete darkness, he bent his head, and took full possession of her lips. Unlike the first time, his kiss was soft, sweet, and completely draining, and when he released her mouth, it was with a gentle tug on her upper lip that threatened to turn into an even deeper caress. His eyes glinted down at her and there was the hint of a smile there. "Happy New Year."

Six

It wasn't until two days later that Alana was able to see Damian again. Her schedule had been rigidly set for her for the next week, and it was only due to her insistence that she be allowed some free time that she had managed to ferret out a couple of hours of leisure at all. She'd given Damian a call and he answered the phone sounding distracted and irritable. It was only after he heard her voice that he appeared to relax. He had accepted with only a momentary flash of displeasure the fact that she wouldn't let him have her telephone number. As strange as it seemed, he really appeared to believe that she was married to Harry and, at least for a while, Alana wanted to leave things that way. Men usually became either uncomfortable or avaricious once they found out who she was.

She had her bodyguard, Peters, whom she had sworn to secrecy, drop her at the Pegasus hotel. He had griped at her for the entire time it took to drive from the house that he would probably be dismissed if it ever got out that he'd left her alone in a strange man's hotel suite. Alana had finally compromised, and agreed to let him remain in the parking lot until she was ready to return home.

On her way up in the elevator, she prayed that she would not encounter anyone who would recognize her. If her father found out what she was doing, he was likely to have a stroke.

At her first knock, the door sprang back. It was as though he'd been waiting just behind it. She felt suddenly shy, and avoided his gaze as she entered.

"I thought you were going to call."

"I couldn't get away before now." Her eyes flickered over him. His masculinity was almost overpowering, making the suite suddenly feel much smaller than it was. He was dressed casually in shorts and a cotton tee-shirt which clung to his upper body like a second skin. He seemed to sense her nervousness, and he walked over to a small desk and sat down, the muscles in his thigh bulging as he did.

Alana walked across to the panel of windows and peered out. She needed something to say, and she seized on the first thing that came to mind, since it didn't appear as though he was going to give her any help.

"You can see the Atlantic from here."

He came to stand beside her, and Alana felt a bead of perspiration trickle down her back as the hair on his arm brushed intimately against her skin. She tried to move away without having him notice, but his arm stole around her to rest on the ledge, successfully confining her movements.

"This is the first time I've ever seen a brown ocean." His voice was husky and golden, a bit like raw honey.

Alana gave him a sideways glance. "You've never visited Guyana before?" Again she realized how silly that response was. Of course he'd probably never visited Guyana before. Not many people from North America chose Guyana as a likely vacation spot. But it was hard to concentrate, with him being so close. He looked down at her, and his expression was enigmatic.

"I would have come much sooner had I known you were here. I might even have gotten you before Harry did."

"You're forgetting I was in Britain." Alana wished that he would move away and give her the chance to breathe normally again.

"Ah, yes." His arms moved in closer so that his entire body surrounded her. "Do you believe in fate?"

"No."

"Liar." He bent his head and kissed her neck. It was just a brief meeting of the flesh, but it caused Alana to jump violently. He seemed surprised by her reaction, and he straightened away from her with a puzzled frown. "You behave like a woman who's not accustomed to being kissed."

Alana made use of that momentary withdrawal to put some space between them.

"Damian, I just came here to talk, nothing else. Do you understand?"

His face settled into a sardonic mask. "Talk? I thought we understood each other. Harry doesn't satisfy you; if he did, you wouldn't be here. Let's be honest about what we both want. I don't enjoy playing games."

Alana felt the blood slowly leave her face. How dare he speak to her like that, as though she were a common trollop? Her eyes glittered with anger. Without a word, she walked across to where she'd slung her handbag and snatched it from its perch.

His voice stopped her halfway to the door. "Where are you going?"

She wasn't going to answer him. She had let her intense desire for freedom, and a few hormones, cloud her ability to see him for the sort of man he really was. A lothario who had no compunction against having an illicit affair with another man's wife.

"If you leave now, I won't ask you back."

The conceit of him, Alana fumed silently. She

wrenched the door open, and was taken completely by surprise when it was whipped from her grasp and slammed shut. He had moved so quietly that she'd been unaware of his approach. He leaned back on the door and slid his hands into the pockets in his shorts.

"Let me out," Alana said seethingly between clenched teeth.

He returned her stare, giving no indication that he intended to do anything of the sort. "So," he said with a slow drawl, "we'll talk."

"It's too late for that. You don't interest me any longer."

"Really?" He ran a forefinger down the length of her arm and watched in satisfaction as a trail of goose pimples appeared in its wake.

Alana turned away from him. She hated to see the knowing look in his eyes. It wasn't fair, the way he could make her feel. And the terrible thing about it was that he seemed all too aware of the devastating effect he had on her.

She looked around in desperation. There had to be something else they had in common besides a wildly inflammable attraction for each other.

Her eyes fell on a small bookshelf that was lined with several thick volumes. She walked across and lifted one from its perch. It was by one of her favorite authors, and she turned back to face Damian, her anger all but forgotten. "You read D.C. Lynch, too," she said, a little smile turning up the corners of her lips.

"Remember, I started telling you about him in Trinidad? Why didn't you tell me that you were a fan, too?"

Damian shrugged. "I'd other more interesting things on my mind."

He hadn't moved away from the door; it was as though he were afraid that she might make a sudden dart for freedom if he relinquished his post.

Alana flipped through the pages of the tome, and she noticed that he had moved silently away from the door and was now watching her with a brooding intensity. She continued talking, trying to re-establish a sense of normalcy.

"In this one he discusses the diaspora of Africans from ancient time to the present, and compares the phenomenon with that of the mass exodus and dispersion of Jews after the end of the Babylonian captivity."

Damian looked at her for a moment, a hint of real interest on his face.

"Did you read all of it? That was one of his earlier books, and it tends to get bogged down in the middle with a lot of philosophical ramblings."

Alana curled up on the sofa and warmed to her subject. At Oxford, when she had not been working in the laboratory, she had found it intellectually refreshing to immerse herself in the many works of Lynch. She probably owned most of his books. They always offered a unique and insightful perspective on the world. He wrote with the conviction of an Alex Haley and the shocking clarity of W.E.B. Dubois. He was brilliant, and she couldn't say enough about him.

An hour later, she had kicked off her shoes and was curled like a little kitten into the nook of the sofa. Her head hung over the side as she defended Lynch's position in his latest novel. She was quite adamant about the fact that this latest book would be the one to capture the coveted Pulitzer, but Damian seemed to feel differently. In fact, he was doing an excellent job at tearing the work apart, pointing out flaws that Alana thought were so minuscule as to be totally unimportant.

"You're just being too nitpicky," Alana said, sitting up with a sudden flourish. "You'll never understand what it's like to be a great writer. Lynch is a man with a poetic soul. A deeply sensitive man who understands the imperfections of the human condition." Her eyes glazed over for a second. "After I've read one of his books, I feel as though he's taught me a little bit more about life, a lot more about myself."

"Anyone could do that," Damian said with a mocking lift of his eyebrows.

Alana sucked her teeth, making a hissing sound that was typically West Indian. "It's pointless. A man like you would be totally oblivious to the true essence of Lynch's nature. I know exactly what he's like. He's kind, and generous, and deeply passionate about everything he does." Damian stood, and stretched, his long muscular body curving backward like the tight arc of a bow.

"You're a hopeless romantic." He stretched his hand out to capture hers. "All this talk about Lynch has worn me out. Let's go for a walk along the sea wall. The breeze at this time of the day is fantastic."

Alana looked at him, and realized with a distinct feeling of disappointment that he was not a very intellectual man. He was handsome, and could be entertaining, but not much else. He was like an empty package with colorful wrapping on the outside.

She stood and smoothed the creases from her trousers.

"I should really be getting back now. It's almost dark, and I'll be missed."

A muscle ticked in Damian's jaw, and Alana saw the flash of some nameless emotion in his eyes.

"A few more minutes won't make that much of a difference." He massaged her palm with the pad of his thumb. "Come with me . . . please." That little word made what would have been a command almost an entreaty, and Alana was momentarily startled. She never would have thought it possible.

* * *

They left the hotel and cut across a patch of green to the sea wall. The sky was beginning to darken, and the first stars twinkled down at them. Damian had captured her hand in his strong grip, and they walked hand in hand in companionable silence. Out of the corner of her eye, Alana could see that Peters was following them. He kept at a discreet distance, so Alana tried to pretend that he wasn't there at all. The evening was so beautiful, and life seemed completely fresh and new. She was almost able to imagine that they were just another couple out for a stroll in the gathering dusk.

The wind picked at her wavy tresses, whipping them across her face, and she brushed the strands away with a careless gesture. A beatific smile curved her lips. Damian looked down at her, and there was a strange light in his eyes. "You look like a kid in a candy store. Doesn't dear Harry go for walks with you? Or is he too busy?"

Alana didn't answer him for a minute. Instead, she stared out at the glistening body of water that was getting darker by the second. The thought occurred to her again as it had in Trinidad. Maybe she should let him know that she wasn't really married. Her brother certainly seemed to be a thorn in his flesh. She looked up at him, considering it. There was a deep smile in his eyes, and her lips curled in response. No. Telling him would only complicate things. He was only visiting Guyana, after all. And this relationship was to be a cotton candy one. Sweet, but definitely not meant to last.

He was still looking at her, waiting for a reply. She forced herself to focus. She would have to choose her words with great care.

"Harry is very ambitious. He needs to be able to live

up to his father's expectations of him . . . so he doesn't go on many walks."

Damian was silent for a brief moment, as though he were in deep thought. "The son of a politician?"

"Yes."

Her abrupt answer brought his eyes swiveling to her face. "You don't like talking about him?"

"Who?" She was instantly nervous, wondering if he was just playing a game of cat and mouse with her, if he really knew who her father was, and that Harry was her brother.

"Your husband's father."

"No." She relaxed again. "I'd really rather not talk about him at all, if you don't mind."

Damian's large shoulders moved in a slight shrug. "I don't mind. I'm much more interested in the son than in the father."

Alana bit the inner corner of her lip. She knew exactly what was coming.

And when he said, "Tell me about you and Harry," she was prepared. With only a very slight pause, she plunged in, keeping her explanations simple, but still convoluted enough to keep him guessing. They had met in Britain. A whirlwind courtship had seen them married. She spoke of Harry's many infidelities. His possessiveness. Her dissatisfaction with the marriage. Her many requests for a divorce. His refusals and threats.

When she was through, her hands were trembling. She had listened to herself talk, and was secretly appalled by the entire fabrication and the ease with which she had told it. Damian said nothing for a long while, and she was glad. They walked a fair distance down the concrete wall that formed a barrier between the land and the ocean before Alana spoke again. She looked down the beveled concrete ledge to where the water lapped below. She was anxious to talk about something safe.

"It's high tide right now, but sometimes you can walk all the way out to where that pier ends." She pointed to a wooden walkway that extended quite a distance out.

Damian tightened his grip on her hand. He appeared to have lost interest in Harry for the moment. "Strange how brown the water is. I always thought it would be green, or blue." His eyes glittered down at her, and Alana suddenly found that she had very little interest in the color of the ocean.

"Silt," she said. He had turned to face her, and he seemed mysterious and exciting in the moonlight. "Silt from the Amazon River makes the Atlantic in this part of the world brown." Her voice tailed off as she realized that he had about as much interest in the color of the ocean as she did.

"Very interesting . . . Doctor Britton," Damian said softly, and he pulled her completely into his arms.

Alana felt a brief surge of embarrassment. Peters was somewhere behind them, observing her every move. She hoped he would not think that Damian was behaving in a threatening manner.

She watched the slow approach of Damian's mouth. She could feel the waves of heat pulsing from him, sense the hard vitality in the way his muscles bunched and relaxed. When he was very close, his head blocking out the moonlight, she closed her eyes. Her sigh filled his mouth, and a shudder ran through him. His kiss deepened to passion immediately, and her hands clung to his broad back, as she gave herself up to the deep pleasure of his kiss. They stood for several minutes, locked in each others' arms, oblivious to the snickers of passersby.

When he raised his head, he seemed reluctant to release her. His arms gathered her closer still, tucking her head beneath his chin and gently massaging her back. Alana's heart beat hard and heavy in her chest. She was certain that he could feel the frantic knocking as she stood closer to him than she'd ever been to any other man. His mouth brushed her ear, and a convulsive shiver went through her as the hairs of his mustache glided across the sensitive skin.

"I want you," he muttered into her hair, rubbing his nose along the silky strands and inhaling the delicate fragrance. "Leave Harry and live with me."

Alana jerked away from him, a sudden movement that caused him to loosen his hold on her. She could see the fierce desire glittering in his eyes, and she turned away from him. What she felt was almost strong enough to make her cast everything to the wind, and face the consequences of her actions after she had purged this madness from her system. But she couldn't. The scandal would be terrible. Her parents would be crushed. They would never understand. Harry, her closest ally, her partner in crime . . . she didn't even want to think what his reaction would be.

She turned back, her eyes blown dry by the wind. Damian had observed her struggle in silence, not touching her, but somehow willing her to say yes. His stillness signaled his unease. It was there in the tight lines of his face and in the rigid way he held himself. She found his eyes in the darkness. They were beautiful eyes, deep and strangely compelling, passionate eyes.

"I can't."

He stepped forward, then made a visible effort to restrain himself. "I know this can't be easy for you. Hell, it's caused me enough sleepless nights"—he gave a harsh laugh—"and I'm not married."

His arms were around her again, his lips on her neck. "I never would've considered having an affair with a married woman before." He gave her neck a slight nip.

"I thought that sort of behavior was beneath me. But you're not happy with him, and . . . God, I just can't seem to stop this . . . this fever. Help me, Lani."

Alana jumped as the pet name Harry had given her rumbled as easily as silk from Damian. How had he known to call her that? She was going up in flames again, and rational thought was beginning to recede to the outer reaches of her consciousness. She couldn't let him go. Not yet. Not until. . . . until what? She didn't know exactly. But until something gave way. This sort of feeling didn't last forever. She knew that. She was a scientist. Trained to be analytical, logical. Mind was stronger than matter. This wasn't real, what she was feeling. It was just . . . just a combination of chemical reactions that caused the mind to fog and the skin to crave his touch. It was nothing more than the primitive need of all species to propagate. Darwin's theory of natural selection. Survival of the fittest, and, Lord, was he fit. The way his body felt—warm and hard. The length of his arms, the touch of his lips, the light in his eyes that seemed to speak to her soul.

"Can we take it slowly?"

He gave a soft chuckle of triumph. "As slowly as you like."

When Alana got home, she felt strangely out of sorts. It was the kind of feeling you got after winning the lottery. A sort of euphoria, tempered by the niggling doubt that maybe, just maybe, it wasn't really true. She was excited and jumpy. Suddenly she found herself looking forward to tomorrow with eagerness—with a thirst for life and all it had to offer—as she had never done before. She would have to be very careful, though. She had already sworn her bodyguard to secrecy, and knew that he could be trusted. It was common knowl-

edge that her father wanted her to marry another Guyanese. He would never approve of Damian. For one
thing, he was not an intellectual. Maybe he didn't even
have a college degree. He appeared to be fairly well-off,
but that alone would not satisfy her father. He was a
darling man, and she loved him dearly, but about certain things, she knew from experience, he would not
be budged. She wished that she might confide in her
brother, as she usually did, but Harry had taken an instant dislike to Damian, and vice versa.

The next few days were the most trying. She had to
convince her mother that she was certainly not coming
down with some dreaded illness. She had sworn off
making public appearances altogether. Her father in-
evitably became just as concerned, and it took some
doing to convince him that her desire to have a schedule which she herself would set was due only to the fact
that she needed a social life outside the political arena.
In the end, it was only Harry who regarded her comings
and goings with veiled suspicion. Her parents didn't
question her movements, but she could see that they
were beginning to wonder what she was up to.

It was a full week after she had begun seeing Damian
regularly that Harry came to her suite. She hadn't spoken to him in a few days, and she looked up with a
pleased smile when he entered. She'd been getting
ready to go to a play at the Cultural Centre. Damian was
meeting her there.

Harry flung himself into a chair and watched her
moodily as she got ready. She was partially into a black
crushed-velvet dress with a diamantine clasp at the
waist. The zipper lolled open at the mid-section of her

back, and she struggled to pull it all the way. Harry walked across and yanked it up. Alana met his eyes in the mirror and knew, without asking, what this visit was all about.

"Why him, Alana?" His voice was terse, and filled with resentment. She noted, with a worried frown, that he'd just called her by her full name, something he hadn't done in years.

Alana wished she could make him understand, but trying to explain would be embarrassing and complicated.

"He's really not as bad as I'd thought." She turned to her brother, an earnest expression on her face. "If you gave him a chance, you might learn to like him, eventually."

"You do realize what he's after, don't you?" he said harshly, his mouth a hard, stubborn line. Alana felt a tide of heat flood her face. Yes, she knew very well what Damian Collins was after, but to say such a thing to her brother might just provide the spark that ignited the already smoldering fuse.

"Why don't you like him, Harry? You only met him once. And you're usually such a fair person. To hate him on sight is ridiculous, and just not like you at all."

He turned away for a moment, his brows puckered in a frown. "He's not right for you."

Alana dabbed a trace of lipstick across her lips. "Not right? You mean because he's not Guyanese?"

"Because he's outside your social bracket. He's beneath you . . ." He stopped when he heard Alana's shocked gasp.

"Harry, you're a snob." She said it with an expression of deep horror on her face.

Harry spun around, his eyes blazing. "I am not a snob. There are just certain conventions that are always observed by people like us."

"People like us? You mean people of African descent?"

"Don't get smart with me. You know exactly what I'm getting at."

Alana slipped her lipstick into her clutch purse. Her fingers trembled slightly, and she was afraid that, if she didn't leave now, she might say something that could ruin the close relationship between her brother and herself. She felt strangely chilled by his words. She'd always thought that they were so much alike. Never would she have thought him capable of such ridiculous notions. Her father had taught them both to be down-to-earth and in touch with reality. To accept public office was to accept the fact that you were now a servant of the people. Not, as her brother seemed to think, a member of an elite bourgeoisie.

"I have to go." Her voice was stiff, and she didn't think that she could talk to him for much longer without exploding.

In the car, she felt the sting of tears behind her eyes. She and her brother never, ever fought. Now, because of Damian, their relationship was becoming strained.

After the play was over, Damian took her back to his suite at the Pegasus for a nightcap. Alana was constantly aware of the presence of her bodyguard. He always kept two cars behind, but there was not much traffic on the roads, and the black sedan seemed to stand out like a sore thumb. Once or twice, she noticed that Damian glanced into his side-view mirror, and she wondered if he knew that they were being followed. At the hotel, he parked the car and helped her out. His eyes burned into hers, and Alana wondered at the wisdom of having accepted his offer of a nightcap before going home. At the entrance to the suite, she stood back while he opened the door. He ushered her inside, then began flicking on lights. Alana sat on a love seat, and watched him as he walked about the room. He looked elegant, powerful, and sexy, all at once. It was difficult for her to understand why he would still be unmarried. Physically, he was everything most women would find irresistible. He turned back to her with a smile hidden in the depths of his eyes. It was as though he'd been aware of her scrutiny, and was deeply pleased by it. He sat beside her, trailing one long arm along the back of the chair. His fingers stole into her hair, gently tugging at the strands.

"Why are you so quiet tonight? Had a fight with Harry?"

Alana started. She was just beginning to realize how remarkably perceptive he was.

"Yes." She loved the feel of his hand in her hair. He was massaging her scalp now, with slow, unhurried strokes of his hand.

"Come here." His hand slid from her hair to urge her closer so that her head rested on his shoulder. He looked down at her, and Alana shuddered, moved by the deep desire in his eyes. His voice was warm and resonant, but she felt no apprehension when he touched her, only a feeling of being complete, of finally finding that part of her that had always been missing.

The thought of how deeply she was becoming involved shook her, and she reached up a tentative finger and traced it across his lips. She felt sure that he stopped breathing while her hand made its first willing exploration of his face. Her fingers ran over his broad, intelligent forehead, stopped to gently stroke the thickness of his eyebrows, then slid down over strong, sculpted cheekbones that spoke volumes of his proud heritage. They finally came to rest once again on his lips, where they poised, trembling. His hand came up to cradle hers, and he pressed a kiss to the center of her palm.

"Damian?"

"Uhmm?" His voice was a husky rumble that vibrated from his chest.

"How long are you going to stay?"

His body stilled for an instant, then she felt him relax again.

"In a hurry to get rid of me?"

She sat up and looked at him. "No. It's just that . . . well, I wondered if you were going to stay for a while?"

He gazed at her for a second, then stood, his expression pensive.

"I'll stay for as long as my schedule permits."

He was shutting her out again, Alana realized. He clammed up in an instant as soon as she started asking questions about him.

His eyes were on her again, caressing, seductive.

"Are you ever going to be my lover?"

Alana blinked in confusion. Wasn't he being rather selfish, expecting her to leave her nonexistent husband to have a short-lived affair with him, after which he would be perfectly willing to move on to whatever it was he would be moving on to?

"You promised to go slowly with me, Damian. You said you understood that our relationship would be complicated."

He frowned. "It's been almost two weeks. Isn't that slow enough for you? Why do women always make such a big thing about sex?"

"You're forgetting that I'm supposed to be married." Her voice was raised a few semitones higher than normal, and he shot her an amused glance.

"*Supposed* to be married?"

Alana groaned inwardly. She should have known that he would pick up on that little misplaced word.

"You know what I mean."

"Do you still love him?"

His question startled her and, for a moment, she wasn't sure how to respond. She decided that the best defense would be attack.

"You don't believe in love, so why talk about it?"

His brows snapped together in a forbidding line. "We're talking about you, not me."

She sighed, then opted for the truth. "Harry and I are closer than most people usually get. He can be difficult sometimes, but I will always love him."

A pulse began to tick along Damian's jawline, and the expression in his eyes hardened. "So why do you need me?"

"I don't know why." Alana stood. They were on the verge of having a fight, and having two disagreements in one evening was more than she could handle.

He grabbed her by the arms, forcing her to look at him. "I'll tell you why. There's something between us that you've never had with another man."

When she turned her head away, he shifted it back, his fingers gripping her chin. "That's right. Can Harry make you feel this?" He bent his head to take her lips in a kiss that caused her to cling to him.

"Or how about this?" He feathered tiny kisses down the bridge of her nose, leaving her hanging as he paused deliberately above her mouth. Her hands tightened, forcing his head down to her. His laugh was smothered by her lips and, when he raised his head, there was grim satisfaction on his face. "I didn't think so."

"I don't want to need you," she whispered.

His hands caressed the sides of her face, his eyes blisteringly intense. "But you do."

"Uhmm." It was her turn to laugh. "And you're not even Guyanese."

His arms kept her in warm contact with his body, and

he looked down at her with sudden laughter in his eyes. "Are you biased?"

"Of course not. But, if I remember correctly, you have some pretty ridiculous notions about West Indian women." She had discovered this during the flight over from London.

He grinned. "You mean about being submissive?"

"Correct."

"Well, maybe that's what some Americans think. But, as you can see, I don't. No one would, after meeting you."

Alana cocked her head and gave him a frank look. "You're not really serious . . . I mean, about Americans thinking that . . . are you?"

He pulled her into a chair and cuddled her against him.

"Many do. Not all, mind you. But I think the ones that do probably haven't had much contact with West Indian women." He paused, his expression growing thoughtful. "But isn't that what lies at the root of all bias?"

"You mean ignorance?"

"Uhmm." His eyes met hers, and it seemed as though, in that moment, a deeper understanding was forged between them. "You're a very interesting lady, do you know that? Harry's a fool not to cherish you. If you were mine, I would."

Alana turned her lips against the strong column of his neck, and she felt him tremble. She was his. She was his, but he could never know it. She had waited too long to tell him that her marriage was a lie and that Harry was her brother. If she told him now, the closeness that was beginning to develop between them would be shattered forever, in the worst possible way. He would no longer trust her. And a relationship without that very crucial ingredient was no relationship at all.

He seemed to sense her disquiet, and he shifted so

that he might see her face. His eyes were kind, and there was a tenderness there. She wanted to tell him, but she couldn't. Instead she asked something that had been bothering her for quite a while.

"Damian . . ."

"Yes?" He kissed the sensitive skin just beside her ear.

"Are you an American by birth? Or did your family move there when you were a child?"

His eyes glowed at her. "Is it my accent that has you a bit confused?"

Alana nodded. "Yes. Also the way you express yourself. Sometimes you sound very West Indian."

He smiled. "My parents were West Indian. That could have something to do with it. But my sister and I were born in the U.S. Also, I've traveled a lot. Britain. The Caribbean. Africa. Maybe I've picked up certain expressions, here and there."

Alana nodded, and snuggled closer. That made sense. She felt more comfortable now, knowing a little more about him. He had opened the door on his life a crack, and that in itself made her happy.

They lay for a while in companionable silence, and Alana forced her mind to go blank. She didn't want to think about the future, the time when he would be gone. She just wanted to exist in this warm moment, lying in the arms of the man who had brought her this deep feeling of fulfillment, of completeness.

"Hey, you're not going to sleep on me, are you?" He tickled her ear, and Alana murmured a protest. It was so comfortable and safe, being here with him, that she was pretty close to slumber.

She opened sleepy black eyes, and she felt a tremor go through him.

"Stay with me tonight?"

Alana glanced at her watch. It was almost midnight. She didn't want to go, but knew that she couldn't stay, because, if she did, Damian would surely discover that she couldn't ever have been married.

"Damian . . ."

"I know. You can't stay." He sat up. "I have something for you."

Alana's eyes narrowed in suspicion, and he laughed.

"Besides that. Wait here . . . or . . ." A note of wicked mischief crept into his voice. "You can come with me, if you prefer."

Alana smiled. "I'll take the first option."

Damian disappeared into the bedroom, then returned shortly. In his hands, he held a brown package. He thrust it at her, then stood back to watch her reaction to his gift. Alana tore away the paper. It was a bound volume by Lynch, her favorite author. She looked up at him, her eyes shining.

"This is his very latest. How did you get it? It's not even in our bookstores yet."

Damian shrugged, "I picked it up in Trinidad, in a bookstore there. I thought that, since you seemed to enjoy his work so much, you might like to have it."

Alana flipped the front cover open. He had signed it, simply, "Damian."

Alana crossed the distance separating them, and placed an exuberant kiss on his lips. He returned it, deepening the caress into one infinitely more satisfying.

That night, Alana had happy dreams. She couldn't believe that this was actually happening to her. She had almost given up hope of finding a man who wanted her just for herself. She placed the book Damian had given her on the small nightstand by her bed, and just before she drifted off to sleep, she stroked the smooth hardness of its cover. It was the next best thing to having Damian beside her.

* * *

The next morning, she went to interview for a job as a chemistry professor at Bishop's High School. The interview process was a mere formality, since her qualifications were more than were necessary for the job. Afterwards, she was given a guided tour of the school. There were seven grade levels, each called a form. Children entered form one, on the average, at age eleven, and graduated school at eighteen when they passed their "A" level examinations in Upper Six. Alana was to teach the third formers chemistry. This had been her choice, since she firmly believed that, when children were learning a subject for the first time, their understanding of it should be thorough. This would provide a strong foundation on which they could build.

She was taken back to her childhood as she was led from classroom to classroom. The green uniforms, the bright eager faces. The popular girls, the studious ones, the shy ones who fell into a curious no-man's land, the cool guys, the ones who thought they knew it all. They were all there, and she was itching to teach them, to see the faces light up with wonder and understanding as she set a new generation of young Guyanese children on the footpath to success. She was needed here. This was her country, and she could never leave. Its future depended on professionals like herself.

She needed to share these thoughts with someone, and she thought of Damian. And with that thought came a deep pain, because she knew that sometime in the not too distant future she would no longer be able to share anything with him. He would leave, because he had to, and she would stay, because she was home.

Seven

Damian moved from the Pegasus Hotel two weeks later. He rented a small white brick cottage on a quiet street in Llamaha Gardens. It was a picturesque location, and Alana loved it on sight. It was cozy and intimate, its view shaded from the road by a colorful mêlée of white and red hibiscus bushes. There was a huge, leafy mango tree in the yard. Standing at the bedroom window, you could lean out and pick fruit from the tree. And, in the evenings, when the sun began to set and a pink flush stretched across the sky, the wind would whisper in a special way through the trees, picking off leaves and hibiscus heads, and shaking ripe fruit from the laden branches. It was a perfect little house. After the first week, Damian settled in nicely. Alana spent all her free time with him. Sometimes she even brought her schoolwork over with her and marked papers and prepared lectures while Damian worked. He had turned the second bedroom in the cottage into a sort of study. He was not as evasive now when Alana questioned him on the nature of his work, but she still wasn't completely clear on what it was that he did for a living. He was an entrepreneur, he'd disclosed one evening when she'd enquired about it. She'd supposed that he was some sort of businessman, because he had a computer set up, and many times when she arrived he would be on the phone. But since there were many things about herself which she could not disclose to him, she tried to harness her curiosity, and accept the little that he told her about himself and his work.

One day in late January, Alana arrived with a bulging satchel filled with test papers which she had to grade before the next day's class. Damian opened the door, and his eyes lit up when he saw her. She placed the bag at her feet and gave him a radiant smile. In the last month, he had exercised remarkable restraint. He had promised not to pressure her into giving anything more than she was willing to give, and he had kept his word. Only occasionally, when he thought that she was unaware of his scrutiny, would she notice that look of unbridled hunger in his eyes.

He closed the door behind her, and she stepped into his arms. This was perfectly natural for her now; she no longer felt embarrassed by the depth of emotion she experienced when he held her. He folded her to him, and she gave herself up to the delicious sensation of having his mouth on hers.

"How is dear Harry?"

His usual question—and Alana pushed the quick stab of guilt she felt to the back of her mind as she gave her usual response. It couldn't be helped now. It had been just a little lie in the beginning, something said in the heat of the moment. Something that had made sense then, but now the situation had become much more convoluted. Her brother still had not fully forgiven her for having anything to do with Damian, and the man in question was only cooling his heels and not pressing her for an intimate relationship because he thought she was married.

Alana placed her bag on the small desk beneath the

window where she normally worked and began unloading her papers. Damian came to stand beside her, and then she was forced to stop what she was doing when he sat on the desk and pulled her into the V made by his legs.

"Do you have to do that now?" Alana ran her fingers up the smooth, hard muscles of his arms. "It'll only take me about an hour. Then I'll be all yours."

There was a flicker of emotion in his eyes, then he said, with a wry twist of his lips, "You have never been 'all mine.'"

Alana felt her heart turn over because of the bleak expression on his face and, before she could stop herself, the words were out.

"But I will be."

There was a flash of molten desire in his eyes, and he pulled her closer. His lips curved into a smile, and their faces were just inches apart. "Anytime soon?"

"It's not going to be as simple as you think. There're people to consider. I have certain responsibilities that I can't just walk away from."

He stroked her hair, his eyes tender. "I understand that. I know it's selfish of me to ask this much of you when there's little that I can give you in return."

"I don't need material things, Damian. I know you're not rich."

"That's not exactly what I meant. You asked me once why I'd never gotten married, and I told you that I thought marriage was inconvenient. Well, I still think so." He stared directly into her eyes, and Alana felt something shrivel and die inside her at the ruthless resolve on his face. "I'll never get married. I want you to understand that up front."

Alana turned away from his probing gaze. Tears were clamoring at the backs of her eyes, and she didn't want him to see that she was at all affected by what he'd just said. He was a hard man, a selfish man, and she loved him, and, God, she hated him, too.

His hands were on her shoulders, and she shook her head, not trusting her voice, when he asked her if there was something wrong. Couldn't he tell what was wrong with her? Was he blind? Maybe Harry was right. She didn't understand men like him, who took the act of lovemaking so lightly. It should mean something, shouldn't it? There should be some feelings involved.

"Lani, I thought you understood how I felt all along. I don't mean to hurt you, hmm?" He kissed the side of her neck. "You and I understand what passion is. You're not a silly little virgin, with crazy romantic notions of how it is between a man and a woman."

"Do you have something against virgins?" she questioned in a strangled voice.

He chuckled, a deep sound that sent an involuntary thrill through Alana.

"I hope I never run into one of them. Getting rid of a virgin is like trying to get chewing gum off the bottom of your shoe. They invariably imagine that they're in love with you, whatever that means."

The chill that was creeping up her body had stilled her tongue, making it sluggish and heavy. Alana knew she was being silly, she knew that she should be able to shrug their relationship off with as much nonchalance as he was apparently able to have. It shouldn't mean any more to her than it did to him. But it did mean more, and it hurt that it meant nothing at all to him. She was nothing more than something he desired and was willing to go the distance to have. Like an expensive car, or some other possession that you used, then discarded when the novelty of it had worn off.

"What would you do if you did run into a . . . virgin?" she already knew what his answer would be, but she wanted to hear him say it. She needed to hear him say it. Maybe then her foolish heart would be willing to relinquish him, and let him get on with the things he considered important in life.

"It's not likely that I'll ever be presented with that dilemma. Times have changed."

"But if you did?" she persisted.

He stood, hands shoved deep within his pockets. In the gathering dusk, his face appeared cold, and completely devoid of all emotion. "I'd run like hell."

Eight

Alana spent most of that night sleeping fitfully. Where was the independent girl of one and a half months ago? The girl who had calmly walked out of that airport in Trinidad and Tobago, knowing that she probably would never see Damian Collins again. How could it be that he'd become such an integral part of her life in so short a period of time? Was it just that she was lonely, and she was blowing a physical attraction way out of proportion? Was it only infatuation that she felt for him? Didn't love take time to grow and blossom into something strong and good that lasted a lifetime?

She picked up the smooth leather volume by Lynch which Damian had given her, and after half an hour of the author's solid, objective style, Alana felt much better. She always did after reading Lynch; his words had always had a calming effect on her. She would think things through as calmly and rationally as Lynch did. She turned off her light, and lay back, staring into the darkness. She did not love Damian Collins. She repeated this until her eyelids sagged shut in exhaustion.

February rolled in with all the splendor and verve typical of that time of year. Most of the fruit trees were in bloom and, on any afternoon, you could take a stroll down to Stabroek Market, and have your pick of a large selection of the juiciest fruit. There were mangoes and star apples to be had, bunches of jamoon that were so purple and sweet that they appeared almost black in color, water coconuts, and long joints of refreshing sugarcane.

It was Saturday, and Damian had convinced Alana to go with him while he explored the open-air market, which sold everything from fresh seafood and vegetables to clothes and notebooks. As they walked along hand in hand, with a huge wicker basket slung across one of Damian's strongly muscled arms, Alana was aware of feeling very conspicuous. Americans always created a stir whenever they were spotted in the market. They were different. They usually wore very colorful shirts and long-legged shorts. The average Guyanese could pick an American out with ease, simply by observing the demeanor and manner of dress. It was often a source of great amusement for the seasoned vendors to attempt to bargain with them. They were either appallingly naive, and willing to pay exorbitant prices for the smallest purchase, or they appeared to think that the merchant did not understand English.

Everything about Damian screamed American. He was not patronizing, but his apparel was amusing. He had come to the market dressed in a red Hawaiian print shirt, Bermuda shorts, and, to crown it all, he was toting a large basket which he had slung across one arm. This was a most un-Guyanese thing to do.

Amusement rippled down the stalls as they passed, and Alana felt that it was only a matter of time before someone recognized her. The fact that Peters was also in tow, dressed in the traditional shirt-jac, wasn't helping matters much, either.

Damian stopped at a stall to investigate the long
strings of live crab that were strung in bunches along
the inside of a large metal drum, and Alana peered with
interest at the struggling creatures. They were huge
crustaceans, with large scaly backs and huge pinchers.

"Do you like these?" Damian was asking her, and
Alana wrinkled her nose at him.

"They're alive."

Damian gave her a tolerant smile. "They won't be for
long. I learned to cook them when I spent a short time
in Jamaica. You break the feet, then drop them into a
pot of boiling water. Kills them instantly."

Alana shuddered. "That's horrible. I couldn't eat
them after torturing them like that."

Damian replaced the string in the drum and slung
an arm about her shoulders. As they walked on, he
looked down at her with a quizzical expression on his
face. "You know, it's strange that you don't know how
to cook. Most West Indian women are right at home in
the kitchen."

"There you go with the stereotypes again," Alana
said, forcing herself to remain calm. He was just being
naturally curious. "Besides, there are a couple of things
that I can cook. I just don't do it that often, that's all."

His eyebrows raised at her. "A couple of things? Like
what? Boiled eggs and toast?"

Alana grimaced at him. "Very funny. I make a mean
aloo choka, and my coo-coo isn't bad, either."

A slight frown creased his forehead. "Aloo what?"

Alana giggled. "Aloo choka is a traditional Guyanese
dish. Aloo means potato in Hindi, and choka is par-
boiled saltfish crushed with potato and yams. Delicious." Her eyes smiled up at him. "So, do you want to
know what coo-coo is?"

He pinched the tip of her nose. "I already do, sweetheart."

Her hand came up to intertwine with the one he had draped over her shoulder. "I bet you don't."

"What do I get if you're wrong?"

"A kiss?" she asked, her eyes alight with wicked humor.

"You're a hard woman, Alana Britton. But I'll accept your challenge. Tonight I'll cook you a dinner that you won't forget in a hurry."

And he did, much to Alana's surprise. He was well versed in the kitchen. Within an hour, he had prepared the coo-coo, which was cornmeal and okra, boiled in butter and served with liver. Alana prepared the aloo choka, and emptied a couple of bottles of ginger beer into a jug. When everything was ready, Damian pushed a table next to the small window in the dining room and they sat down to enjoy the meal.

After dinner, they cuddled into the nook of the solitary sofa and watched old movies. Occasionally, Damian's mouth would wander down the side of Alana's face, and he would press a kiss to the corner of her mouth. The sensation was so pleasingly sensual that Alana found herself waiting impatiently for his next caress. One of his arms lay across her midriff, trapping her intimately against the hard length of his body, and her fingers played with the hairs on the back of his hand.

The feel of his warm body through the thin cotton of his shirt, and the gentle, consistent thudding of his heart, were the best feelings Alana had ever experienced. She had never felt closer to another human being. A wealth of tenderness enveloped her and, unconsciously, she pressed his hand to her breast as she fell into a contented sleep. When she awoke, both his arms were around her, and his face rested on the side of hers. He slept without a sound, and Alana was reluctant to wake him. But she couldn't let Peters spend the night parked in his car. Besides, her parents would be worried, and her brother would seek Damian out, and the outcome of that meeting might not be pretty.

She shifted slightly. "Damian?" His body was almost completely sandwiching hers. He stirred, and his arms tightened, pulling her even closer to him. She shook his arm gently, and she felt his eyes open against her face. He lifted an arm and peered at his watch. "What time is it?"

"One o'clock."

He gave her a slow, sleepy smile that made Alana's heart turn over in her chest. Then he bent and gave her a thorough kiss. When he raised his head, his eyes were filled with a strange light.

"It's good to have you here with me, babe."

Alana smiled. And it was good to be with him. But she would never tell him that now. She didn't want him to think that she was in love with him, because she wasn't. He was just a compatible soul—a kindred spirit—but she didn't love him. She had given herself a stern talking to, and reading Lynch had helped a good deal. What she felt for Damian was nothing more than a strong fascination, a passing fancy. It wouldn't last. In a couple of months, she would be back to her normal, rational self. She stretched up a hand and patted the side of his face. He was still looking at her in that peculiar way, and it was beginning to make her feel a bit nervous.

"I have to go home."

"You said Harry would be working late tonight."

"Not this late."

He released her with marked reluctance, then observed her attempts to smooth the creases from her jumpsuit with a dour expression. "So you'll spend the rest of the night in Harry's arms?"

Alana paused for a moment. He was a very possessive man. Not that she minded terribly—she might even like it, if his possessiveness was the precursor to a stronger emotion—but she knew it wasn't. He was just the kind of man who did not like to share. For a minute, she wondered if she should let him think that she and Harry shared the same bedroom, but then she dismissed the thought as childish.

"Harry and I haven't shared the same room for many years."

At least that was true. She had been afraid of the dark, and she and her brother had shared a bedroom until she was well into her teens.

Alana glanced at Damian, and noticed that his eyebrows had drawn together into a straight black line. "You don't really expect me to believe that your husband has willingly given up his conjugal rights."

"We sleep in separate rooms," Alana repeated, and felt a flood of heat wash her face. She avoided looking at him and, instead, fiddled around for her shoes.

"He's a very strange man. Where does he think you are now?"

"At a girlfriend's house." The lie slid from her tongue a little too glibly, and, for a minute, she was afraid that he was going to question her further.

"Wait a minute." He was suddenly out of his chair, and towering before her. "I'll take you home."

Alana's heart fluttered wildly. This was the first time that he'd ever made such a suggestion. Did he know where she lived? Surely he couldn't, she'd been so careful.

"No." Her quick response did not deter him, and she saw a stubborn glint come into his eyes. She hurried on desperately. "I mean, Harry will be on the lookout for me, and . . ." She gesticulated with her hands.

"Your marriage is a sham," Damian growled, his eyes hard and flintlike. "You told me as much yourself."

Alana blinked at him, panic contracting her throat. "What do you mean?" she wavered.

"What do I mean?" He sounded incredulous. "You sleep in separate bedrooms. You're here with me, and I'm willing to bet that your Harry"—and he spat the name out with a hint of derision in his voice—"knows exactly where you are right now, and he doesn't appear to care. That's what I mean."

Alana's fingers were curled into tight fists, and her nails bit into the soft flesh of her palms.

"I don't want to talk about this, Damian. There are inconsistencies in your life, too, and I don't question you about them."

He appeared to withdraw from her immediately, although there was still a flicker of emotion in his eyes.

"He doesn't deserve you. He doesn't deserve such loyalty. What hold does he have over you? Why won't you leave him if you're not happy?" He was standing directly before her in an instant. "You're not afraid of him?" His voice became laden with aggression. "He doesn't . . . hurt you?"

"Of course not." Alana stared up at him. This was becoming worse by the minute. Why wouldn't he just leave it alone? Why couldn't he accept her explanations?

"Then why? Make me understand."

"Love. I still love him. Something you're incapable of feeling or understanding."

Damian was silent for a long moment, then he handed her the phone. "Call someone and have them pick you up. It's too late to go searching for a taxi."

When she got home, her brother greeted her at the door.

"Where the hell have you been? I thought you'd been kidnapped, or worse."

"I was with Damian, Harry. I am a grown woman."

He followed her up to her suite, and sat on her bed.

"You still haven't forgiven me for those things I said about your precious Damian, have you?"

Alana walked into her bathroom and disrobed quickly, slipping into her old flannel pajamas. She was beginning to feel quite tired, and didn't feel up to discussing Damian with Harry. Their little talks of late always degenerated into arguments whenever they concerned her relationship with Damian.

When she returned to the room, Harry was lying on the bed, staring at the ceiling. Alana felt a twinge of pity, and she went and sat beside him. He took her hand and stared at the lines crisscrossing her palm. "Lani, you never spend any time with me anymore."

A grin spread across Alana's face, and Harry gave her a pained look.

"Harry, you crazy idiot. You're jealous of Damian. That's why you don't like him."

He gave her hand a squeeze. "I am not." He sat up suddenly. "There's just something about him that's not right. I never found out how it was that he came to be at the President's Old Year's Night ball."

"Oh, he explained that to me a while ago," Alana said. "He came as a member of the Trinidadian delegation. Apparently he knew one of the senior officials. And he decided to come along when he saw my name on the guest list."

Harry gave a noncommittal sound. "I still don't trust him. What's he doing in Guyana anyway?"

Alana climbed beneath the covers. "We'll talk about this later. Right now, I have to get some sleep."

He nudged her shoulder, and her eyes popped back open.

"What?" she asked, as her lids sagged shut again.

"You said you wanted us to be friends?"

"Uhmm hmm."

"Well, I'm willing to give him another chance, though I don't think he took to me, either."

"Oh, he hates you pretty much," she mumbled.

"Will you tell me where he's staying?"

Alana forced her eyes open and peered at him. "Why?"

"So I can drop by and extend the olive branch."

"You can't. He still thinks we're married."

"You haven't told him that I'm your brother? What kind of relationship do you have?"

"In the beginning, I didn't want to because . . . well, you know why, and now it's too late. He'd never forgive me."

"So you just intend to go on deceiving him."

"You should be pleased," she snapped, pulling the blanket up over her head. "He'll be gone soon anyway, so it won't matter."

Harry patted the portion of blanket that covered her head. "It's probably all for the best, anyway. Goodnight."

After he had gone, Alana pulled out the red volume by Lynch and read a complete chapter. All for the best; what did Harry know? Tonight, Lynch's words did not soothe her, something that had never happened before. His descriptions of ancient African civilizations swam before her eyes. All she could think of was Damian, and what he was doing right then, and how much she wished that she was free to go to him, curl up in his arms, and let the thud of his heart lull her to sleep.

***

Sunday morning was quiet and peaceful. Alana was up and dressed before anyone was awake. It was normal in the Britton household to sleep until noon on Sundays. At five o'clock, there would be a huge Sunday dinner, and a discussion of politics shortly thereafter.

Today, Alana decided that she would leave a note, skip the usual festivities, and spend the entire day with Damian. She had come to a decision during the night. She would tell him that she wasn't married to Harry . . . that he was her brother. The decision to tell him took a great weight off her shoulders, and she said goodbye to Peters, when he dropped her a block away from the cottage, with a bounce in her step.

She gave the doorbell a solid ring and then stood back to admire the garden. Sunday mornings seemed to have a fresh beauty that was entirely their own. The leaves on the mango trees were a deep glossy green, the delicate hibiscus petals fluttered in the breeze, scattering their orange pollen on the neatly manicured grass, and the sweet fragrance of nature danced and shimmered in the air.

The door behind her opened, and Alana turned with a smile on her face. "Damian . . ." and the words on her tongue stilled. There was a woman standing in the doorway, and she was in the process of belting a satin robe about her obviously naked body.

"Yes? What do you want?" Her voice had a slight edge to it, and Alana's shocked brain registered that she was also American.

"Who are you?" she asked, in a voice that was trembling with a mixture of rage and jealousy.

The woman gave her an assessing glance. "Damian is unavailable right now, so run along." She made as if to close the door, and Alana shoved hard against the lacquered wood, pushing the other woman backward.

She entered the house and made a beeline for the bedroom.

The other woman grabbed at her hand. "Don't disturb him. He's been up all night."

Alana saw red. How dare he go to another woman after spending time with her? After making her think that she was the only one he was interested in? How could he bring another woman into this house, their house?

She turned on the other woman with vengeance in her eyes.

"Take your hand off me." Her voice was cold, and there was a dangerous stillness about her.

"I'm not going to let you wake him up, so if you're one of his one-nighters, I'd suggest that you leave before this gets unpleasant. He has a commitment to me, and I'll be damned if . . ."

She got no further. "Stacy, that's enough." Damian's voice rapped out harshly, and Alana spun to face him. His chest was bare, exposing the glorious growth of black hair to the full view of both women. Alana stared at him, and her throat went dry. There was no shame or apology on his face. She felt tears prick the corners of her eyes, and she turned on her heel and headed for the door. She heard his harsh exclamation, then she was spun into his arms.

"It's not what you think."

She heard the woman called Stacy laugh, and felt a fresh surge of anger.

"Let go of me, Damian. What you do is no concern of mine."

He held her until her struggles ceased, then he said in a husky voice. "She's nothing to me. It's strictly business, between us."

Alana gasped. "You mean she's a . . ."

"No," he said. "She's my business associate."

Alana peered at him doubtfully. "Why is she dressed like that?"

Damian flickered a disinterested glance at the woman, who was now leaning against a wall smoking a cigarette. "I have no idea. She wasn't when I went to bed. Stacy," he growled, "put some clothes on and go back to the hotel. I'll contact you later."

The other woman shrugged, and disappeared into the study. A few minutes later, she re-emerged, fully clothed. She nodded at Damian, and ignored Alana completely. Shortly after, Alana heard the sound of a car starting.

When all was quiet again, Alana realized that Damian's arms were still around her. She looked up at him, and was disconcerted to find that he had been observing her all the while.

"Maybe I'd better go, so you can get some more sleep. She said you hadn't much last night." There was a question in her voice, and Damian answered it with a slight shake of his head. "She arrived shortly after you left. An emergency. We had to work through the rest of the night."

Her mouth rounded in a surprised "O." His lips were temptingly close, and he grinned down at her. "Not what you thought though."

Alana felt embarrassed heat flood her face. "Well, what else could I think? She wasn't even dressed when she answered the door."

"You were ready to fight for me." He sounded pleased.

Alana grinned. "No, I wasn't."

"I heard you," he said, "screaming at the top of your lungs. You woke me up. Thought I was dreaming at first, then I realized it was really you."

"You should go back to bed. You look tired."

He bent his head and kissed her softly on the lips. "Come with me."

Alana yielded to his persuasion for a minute, then she forced herself to think rationally. She had to tell him now that she wasn't married. She would get no better chance. Maybe he might forgive her. Maybe.

"Damian," her voice faltered, and he tilted her chin up so that she was forced to meet his deep black eyes. They were like velvet now, soft and smooth, and filled with passion tempered by tenderness.

"I know. But all I want to do is hold you while I sleep. Nothing else. You trust me, don't you?"

Alana nodded, feeling a deep sinking sensation in the pit of her stomach. He kissed her again. "I've never met another woman like you. So honest . . . innocent and pure somehow. A big change from what I'm used to."

Alana gulped, and he misinterpreted the involuntary motion of her throat as nervousness.

"There's nothing to be worried about. I'll be asleep in five minutes. Come on." He slid his arm around her waist and urged her in the direction of the bedroom.

She couldn't tell him now, not after what he'd just said about honesty, Alana thought. He'd hate her. She almost hated herself.

The curtains were drawn in the bedroom, making the room appear dark and intimate. There were two large pillows, one with a deep indentation. A dark mohair blanket was flung back along with the sheets, indicating the haste with which Damian had left the bed. Alana felt the thud of her heart in her chest. Suddenly her palms were sweating, and the atmosphere in the room seemed to have heated up several degrees. Damian walked to the closet, and pulled out a pair of black pajamas. He turned back to her with a slight question in his eyes.

"You're so small. Do you think these will fit?"

"For me?" Alana blinked at him for a moment. She felt completely out of her element, standing here discussing clothes with a half-naked man—one whom she desired with a burning intensity.

"Well," he said with a considering glance, "you can't sleep in your clothes . . . unless you'd rather nothing at all?"

Alana snatched the pajamas from his hand. "No, these are fine."

She heard his husky chuckle as she scuttled into the bathroom to change. When she returned, he was already in bed, lying propped against the pillows. His eyes made a slow perusal of her from head to toe, and Alana shivered in response to his blatant sensual assault on her body.

"They look much better on you." Alana had rolled the legs up slightly, cinched the drawstring around her small waist, and tied the front of the shirt into a little knot just above her navel.

"I've waited for this moment for a long time," Damian said, his eyes finding hers and holding them. Alana stepped backward a little, her hands coming up as if to ward him off.

"Damian, you said . . ."

"I was just kidding." He patted the bed beside him. "Come on, I need my sleep."

Alana went, on shaky knees. She sat on the bed, and he held out his arms. It occurred to her in that instant that she was getting exactly what she had wished for just the night before. He reached down and pulled the blanket and sheet up over them. The air conditioner blew cool drafts of air across the room, and Alana snuggled into the warmth of his embrace. She looked up into his smiling black eyes, and he looked down at her as if to say, "Now what?"

Her lips curved into a smile. "Go to sleep," she said.

His arms ran caressingly across her back. "Are you sure that's what you want me to do?"

"Very sure."

He gave an exaggerated sigh, and rested his head against hers. In minutes, he was sound asleep, and Alana lay perfectly still in his arms, afraid that her slightest movement might disturb him. Her head rested beneath his chin, and he held her to him as though she were the most important thing in the entire world. The hair on his chest tickled her face, and the subtle masculine aroma that he exuded played havoc with her senses.

Sometime later, his leg slung across her, to pull her in even closer, and Alana felt that surely no feeling on earth could possibly rival this. Finally, she slept too, and didn't awaken until late in the afternoon.

When she awoke, Damian was gone from beside her, and she sat up slowly, slightly disoriented. The door to the bedroom was partially open, and she could hear the sounds of movement coming from somewhere outside. She slid out of bed and padded to the door, just as it was pushed back and Damian appeared. There was a tray in his hand, and a fluted vase filled with dusky-red hibiscus flowers.

"So, you're finally awake. You were out for the count." He placed the tray on the bedside table, and Alana lifted the white linen that covered it.

"Fried fish and breadfruit?" she exclaimed in surprise.

"You like?" he said, lifting his brows and imitating some foreign accent.

"Just my favorite," she responded. Then, with a curiosity which she couldn't quite conceal, "Damian, how is it that you know how to cook all these West Indian dishes? Did your mum teach you?"

"No," he said, pulling her down onto the bed to sit between his legs. "When my mom was alive, I wasn't interested in learning. It's mostly because I've lived all over the world, and I've had to fend for myself. I spent quite a few years in different African countries and, as you know, most West Indian foods have their roots in Mother Africa."

"Uhmm, you're right," Alana said, and opened her mouth to receive a proffered piece of the soft, sweet breadfruit and fish stuffed with hot peppers.

"You know," she said through mouthfuls. "You're a pretty interesting guy."

"And you," he said, pressing a kiss to the side of her neck, "are my very special girl. I don't cook for just anybody."

"No?" Alana asked cheekily.

"No," he said.

After a thoroughly devastating kiss, she asked him to tell her about Africa, and he did, in a way that was so scholarly, and so lyrical, that Alana thought that she might listen to him forever.

Nine

Mashramani in Guyana was a time of celebration and countrywide excitement. The word itself meant freedom, and, on February twenty-third, the entire country exploded with life and color, tramping through the streets in costume behind the calypso caravans and flamboyant floats. It was a celebration of life, of achievement, and, most of all independence from the shackles of British colonialism.

It was a festive occasion, and everyone prepared for it for weeks. There were calypso contests. The best performers would be chosen from these. And the winners would participate in the parade.

On the night before Mashramani, there was a lot of eating, dancing, and general merrymaking. It was like the Mardi Gras of New Orleans, or the Carnival of Trinidad and Tobago.

This year's celebration promised to be the best one yet. Food stands lined the streets, and large areas of Georgetown were blocked to traffic. This would be the first time ever that Alana would actually participate in the fun of "mashing" with the hordes of people who would dance for miles behind the calypso caravans. It was like nothing else, total strangers swaying backward and forward with their hands around each others' waists. She'd seen it from quiet, protected rooms all her life, and had always wished fervently that she could be down on the streets in the mêlée, enjoying the quintessence of what it was to be Guyanese.

This year, finally, she would fulfill that desire. Her parents and Harry were, of course, unaware of her plans. She had chosen the most outrageous costume, with a lot of glittering cloth and a large mask for her face, so that no one would recognize her. She intended to put loads of sparkles in her hair, and dance along the streets with Damian, until they were too exhausted to follow the caravans and swaying masses any farther. Peters, her bodyguard, would also be in costume. Over the weeks, Alana had found him to be very accommodating, and not at all the stiff and unbending soul that she had once thought he was.

The day before Mashramani, Alana carted her costume over to Damian's house and put the finishing touches on it there. She sat on the floor and painstakingly sewed each motif to the soft gauzy material. Her costume was a visual representation of the Guyanese cultural and racial melting pot.

When she had finished, there were beads of perspiration covering her face, and she looked up gratefully when Damian appeared with a pitcher of lemonade. He grinned down at her. "You're definitely not accustomed to manual labor."

Alana pushed the hair back from her face and accepted the proffered glass of drink.

"Well, what do you think?" she asked, after a brief pause.

Damian picked the dress up and gave it a thorough going-over.

"I guess it'll have to do," he said finally. "Let's face it, you're no seamstress, either."

"Oh, you . . ." Alana launched herself at him, tumbling them both backward onto the wide sofa. He grabbed her flailing hands and, between rasping chuckles, kissed each digit. Alana lay astride him, and she reciprocated by kissing each one of his. When she raised her head, he was looking at her with an unfathomable expression in his eyes. He pulled her up so that her mouth was directly above his, then his fingers moved slowly over the bones of her face, caressing each dip and undulation with a whisper-light touch.

"My beautiful girl," he said, with something like wonder in his voice. "If I were a poet, I would write stirring sonnets about you."

"Damian . . ." But whatever she was about to say was suspended, as he turned her expertly. Then his lips were on hers, and it was completely forgotten.

Ten

It was clear and beautiful on Mashramani Day. There were barricades for miles, and huge crowds lining the streets. The food vendors were out en masse. Curry and roti, black pudding, polouri with mango chutney, jamoon sno' cones, and lemon shaved ice. The festive atmosphere and the excitement were contagious.

Damian had parked his car in the center of town and, together, he and Alana walked to the starting point of the parade. The steelbands were already on the trucks, and Alana pointed excitedly at a calypsonian whom she recognized.

"Look, there's the Mighty Sparrow." Damian glanced in the direction which she'd indicated, and waved to the singer, who nodded in return.

"Do you know him?" Alana asked, a little awed by the possibility.

Damian smiled down at her. "You told me that everybody is one big happy family today."

"Well, don't get too carried away," Alana admonished in a tone of mock reprimand.

They walked down the long line of gathering trucks and floats, commenting with interest on the many colorful and imaginative costumes they passed. Quite a few heads turned to follow them as they went by, and Alana decided that maybe it was time to put on her mask.

Damian was dressed like a Guyanese folk dancer in a tie-dye shirt and calf-length frayed pants. He'd also elected to wear a mask. Out of the corner of her eye, Alana could see Peters following them at a safe distance. She had tried to convince him that she would be fine with Damian, but he wouldn't hear of it. He had insisted, and Alana had to admit that he blended right in with everyone else. No one would ever guess that the rather idiotic-looking man dressed in a white flour-bag costume was actually one of the finest security men in the country.

The sun had risen high in the sky, and Alana raised her hand to shield her eyes against the glare. There was so much to be seen. There were many people dressed as various folklore characters. From where she stood, she could clearly make out the "Obeah man," and his counterpart, the "Old Hige"—the Guyanese equivalent of a vampire. She pointed them out to Damian, explaining the superstitions behind each one. He listened to her with rapt attention, and Alana was distinctly pleased that he appeared so enthralled by what was going on.

Suddenly, the steelband started up and the crowd surged forward. The trucks began to move, and Alana felt a wave of excitement wash over her. This was it. The road march was really underway. She grabbed hold of Damian, and showed him how to move his waist in the rolling side-to-side motion known to all West Indians as "wy-nin." There were rows of people in front and behind, and as the music dipped and swayed, the rows tramped forward, then backward, in the typical rhythm of the road march.

Damian got into the swing of things rapidly and, before very long, he was "mashing" like the locals. The calypsonians soon took over from the steelband players, and that was when the crowd really started to sway. Alana was buffeted by the bump and grind of bodies, but Damian kept a firm arm around her waist. At one point, when the crowd was whipped into such a frenzy that Alana lost one of her shoes, Damian lifted her, without chagrin, to sit astride his broad shoulders, and continued to dance unfazed. From her perch, Alana had a bird's-eye view of miles of floats and people. She looked around for her bodyguard, Peters, but in the crush of people it was impossible to tell where he was.

After about two miles, Damian left the parade briefly to buy them both large double-decker ice-cream cones. The vendor didn't seem at all surprised at the sight of Alana sitting on Damian's shoulders. It was Mashramani, and it was understood, almost demanded, that everyone let their inhibitions down and have a good time.

They rejoined the parade, and Alana laughed with delight when Damian lost his ice-cream cone to the jostling crowd. She handed hers down for him to sample, and they shared it together. It was the best fun that she'd ever had in her entire life, and it seemed that Damian was enjoying himself immensely, also. She caught sight of Peters at one point, and another gurgle of laughter pealed from her throat. He had lost both his shoes, the straw hat which had been sitting with a certain distinction atop his head was now barely recognizable, and his pristine white flour-bag costume was now almost black. She tried to attract his attention, but he was involved in a valiant struggle to extricate himself from the clutches of a rather large woman who seemed determined to dance with him, whether he wanted to or not.

It was an hour and a half before they got to the national park, and Alana feigned weariness so that Damian could take a rest. They could always catch up with the parade later if they wanted to.

Damian flopped back on the soft green grass, and

Alana fanned him vigorously with her mask. The sun was blisteringly hot, and he turned toward her to wipe her face free of perspiration.

"Having fun?" he asked, his eyes smiling up at her.

Alana returned his smile, and she hoped that the love she felt for him was completely hidden. "The best time I've ever had. How about you?"

Damian propped himself up on his elbows, and Alana longed to kiss his lips, not once, but over and over again. He pulled a clump of sparkles from her hair, and a shiver went through her as his gentle touch sent tingles all across her scalp.

"You're the best thing that's ever happened to me," he said, a husky note in his deep voice. He pulled her down and, in the middle of the park, amidst numerous picnicking families, he kissed her, and Alana responded to him with unbridled enthusiasm.

When they returned to the cottage in Llamaha Gardens that evening, Alana's face and shoulders were burning slightly, due to over-exposure to the sun, but the minor discomfort was worth the precious memories which she would file away, and cherish for as long as she lived. There was no other man who could make her feel the way Damian did, and definitely none other whom she would care for as deeply. This was love. This was what the poets of the ages had gone to great pains to describe. It was the deep tenderness she felt whenever she saw him. A tolerance for his little quirks. It was soft and sweet, then, just as suddenly, raw and passionate. It was so right, like a comfortable glove, and she yielded herself to it.

It rained all the next day, and Alana called Damian just before noon to let him know that she couldn't see him until Monday. He answered the phone with barely concealed irritation, and sounded quite preoccupied, and not at all upset when Alana told him that she wouldn't be over. In fact, there had been a note of relief in his voice. Alana hung up and went back to preparing her lecture for Monday's classes, mulling over in her mind whether or not Stacy might be with him, and if she really was a business associate, as he'd explained.

She spent the remainder of the day reading the novel by Lynch. She was immersed in the thick of it, and found herself becoming more deeply enthralled by the vivid pictures of ancient African life which the author painted with such precision. At the end of a particularly gripping chapter, Alana rested the book on her knees and stared at the jagged flashes of lightning which lit the dark sky outside her bedroom window. She sincerely wished that she might have a chance to meet Lynch, and discuss his ideas with him. She felt that there was so much that she could learn from him. She had wanted to meet Alex Haley, also, but that had not been possible. She was afraid that the same might apply to Lynch. He was obviously a contemporary of Haley's. He had to be. His vision and understanding of human nature bespoke a certain experience that was only gained through years of living life.

On Monday, she went over to Damian's cottage after school. The front door was slightly ajar, as though someone had recently left in a hurry. She pushed the door and went in, and found Damian seated before his computer in the study.

"Stacy, I told you not to disturb me again."

Alana touched him on the back of his neck, and he turned sharply, his face full of impatience.

"Lani." He seemed surprised to see her, and not altogether pleased.

"I said I would be over today, remember?"

He looked at her blankly for a moment, then apolo-

gized. He rubbed the flat of his palm across his forehead, and he turned away from her to stare out the
window. Alana's brow puckered in a slight frown. What
was wrong? Surely, he hadn't guessed that she was in
love with him. She had been careful not to show it.
They had had a wonderful time on Mashramani Day.
Nothing had gone wrong. And he hadn't questioned
her about Harry in a while, so it couldn't be that.

"Alana, I'm going to have to leave."

The breath paused in her throat. She'd been expecting anything else, but not that. Her hand came up to
press against her mouth, and a shard of pain so deep,
and so painful, tore through her. For a full minute, she
was unable to speak. Tears pricked at the corners of
her eyes, and she fought against the terrifying feeling
of loss which swept over her.

His shoulders were tense, hard, and seemingly un-
yielding. When he turned to her, Alana was grateful
that her face showed no trace of the desperate struggle
which she was waging with herself.

"Nothing to say?" His voice was harsh, almost angry,
as though he blamed her for something.

She took a slow, deep breath, and willed her voice
not to tremble. She would not show him how much he
was hurting her. "I always knew you would leave eventually, but I didn't expect it to be so soon."

He stood looking at her, his face immobile save for
the pulse which was throbbing just below his jawline.

"This situation between you and me, it's no good for
me. I'm beginning to lose my edge."

When she made no reply, he went on. "My work is
very important to me. It must come first, always."

Alana turned toward the window. The mango tree
bowed beneath a gust of wind, and the same scene
which had made her so deliriously happy a few days

before was now etched into her heart with profound sorrow.

He came to stand behind her, and she felt him, even though he did not actually touch her.

"Don't you care, not even a little?" His voice was torn with some raw emotion.

"You want me to beg you to stay?" Alana choked out. "Why should I? You don't need me. You don't need anyone. Just your . . . your damn work. Whatever it is you do."

He was silent for what seemed an eternity, then his hand snaked out and curved around her waist.

"That was true. I never needed anyone before . . . you." He pulled her back against him, and buried his head in her hair. Alana felt her body respond to him, and a tear slipped from the corner of her eye. She wiped it away with a fierce hand. He held her tightly, as though he were attempting to absorb her very essence. She was glad now that she had not let him know that she wasn't married—that she was still an innocent, the very creature he feared the most. She didn't want his pity, by God. She would turn around and walk out of this house, out of his life, with, if nothing else, her pride.

She pulled out of his embrace, and turned to face him, and her heart stopped cold. There were tears in his eyes, and as she watched, stupefied, one large droplet rolled over, and trickled a wet path down his face.

"Damian . . ." She was in his arms again, kissing away the wet from his face. Kissing lips which clung to hers with equal fervor.

"Understand me, Lani, I have to leave you. I don't want to."

None of this made any sense at all to Alana. Why did he have to leave? What was it about her that made working at the cottage so impossible?

"Is it Stacy? Does she want you to leave?"

He held her close. "She does want me to leave here, but she's not the reason. I have to put some distance between us. I can't focus anymore."

"How can you be so selfish, Damian?" She paused and shook her head in bitter realization. "No, it's damn stupid, that's what it is. Damned bloody stupid, and I can't pretend to understand what you think you're doing."

His face tightened for a moment. "If you think I love you, then you're wrong. I don't. I told you I didn't believe in that drivel. It's weak, and I want no part of it."

Alana felt an instant flush of anger. "You're a conceited idiot. And just let me assure you that I am in no danger of falling in love with you either. So, go, if you must. Go tomorrow. Hell, go tonight!"

She grabbed her bag and flounced to the door.

"Alana."

She turned with her hand on the doorknob. He looked suddenly older. "Stay with me tonight? Maybe, if you do, we'll both be able to wipe the slate clean and go on with our lives."

"That's your solution to everything, isn't it? A toss in the hay, and the world's all right again. Is it possible that there could be another man on the face of this earth as shallow and superficial as you are?" She wrenched the door open, and barreled into Stacy.

"He's all yours," Alana said to the other woman.

"Alana!" She heard his heavy footsteps behind her, and heard him growl some expletive at poor unfortunate Stacy.

She was going down the front stairs when he caught up with her. He lifted her bodily, and slung her across a shoulder. She struggled fiercely, and felt a swamping wave of mortification when she caught sight of Stacy's astonished face.

"Damian, put me down," she shrieked. He kicked the front door closed, and kept going.

"Maybe you should do as she says, Damian," Stacy intervened.

"Get out!" he growled in response, and the other woman took one look at his face and hurriedly complied.

Damian strode toward the bedroom, and Alana felt a twinge of something rather like terror. He couldn't be thinking of forcing her. He wouldn't. Would he?

She landed smack on her back on the firm mattress, and she opened her eyes to stare into his deep black ones. She didn't move, and neither did he. They stared at each other like two antagonists, waiting for the other to make the first move. The rigid control which Alana had been exercising suddenly broke, and she rolled onto her side and began to weep. Deep racking sobs were torn from her throat. She heard his concerned murmur, felt his hands reach out to pull her to him, and unashamedly, she cuddled into his embrace and let him comfort her. He muttered husky endearments against her cheek, and rocked her in a back and forth motion that was strangely soothing.

"Forgive me," he said hoarsely. "I never meant to hurt you, Lani."

"But you have," she sobbed.

He nodded. "It's always been like that. Anything I care about, I destroy."

Alana raised her tear-streaked face and looked at him. "Do you care about me?"

His thumb stroked away the wetness. "I don't love you, but I don't want to hurt you, either. I guess I do care about what happens to you." His voice was gruff, but there was also a note of tenderness there.

Alana held his hand. "You're a very difficult man to understand, Damian Collins."

"Not as difficult as Harry, I suppose?"

Alana shook her head. "No. Harry's a sweet and simple guy and, for the most part, we understand each other."

A brief frown passed across his face. "Are you still sleeping in separate rooms?"

"What do you care?" Alana asked, tugging at his shirt collar absently. "You're going to leave, and we'll never see each other again. It doesn't matter what I do."

"Who said anything about not seeing each other again?" He was staring at her as though the realization of that fact had just struck him.

"You did."

He played with a twist of her hair. "Well, you got me all wrong. I fully intend to see you again. We haven't made love yet, and that should be an experience that neither of us forgets in a hurry."

"How can you be so sure? It might be terrible between us." Her eyes flickered up to meet his, and held.

A slow smile stretched his lips, and he stared at her as though he was really seeing her for the first time.

"You know," he said with a hoarse laugh, "you sound exactly like a virgin. But, of course, that's not possible."

"Of course." Alana straightened away from him, and he released her.

"So, when are you going to leave?" she asked, not looking at him. If she did, she just might start crying again. "Or did you plan to disappear without letting me know?"

He sat on the edge of the bed, resting his arms on his knees. The setting sun streamed through the window, bathing the room and him in a soft, golden glow. He turned his head to look at her, and she somehow sensed the conflict that was raging deep within him.

"A month or two. Can't stay any longer than that. Probably the end of April. The trees will be coming into bloom in Pennsylvania then. Great red and gold leaves. A beautiful sight. I wish you could see it."

Alana bit her lip. "That's where you live in America?"

This was the first time he had ever really revealed anything about himself to her voluntarily.

He shook his head. "My sister has a house in Reading. I've never really lived anywhere. Never found a place where I wanted to settle." He gave a harsh bark of laughter. "A free spirit, I guess that's what you'd call me."

Alana touched him, and she felt a little of what he must be feeling. She too had felt restless from time to time, as though she were searching for something which she could not exactly define.

"I wouldn't call you that. You're not free. Until you find whatever it is you're in search of, you'll never be able to call yourself a free spirit."

He stared at her for a long second, as though he were absorbing what she'd just said. Then he nodded, and there was a moment of shared understanding between them.

"You're a very wise woman." He held out his hand for hers. "Let's go for a walk. We can plan how we're going to spend the next month, and enjoy the evening at the same time."

As they walked down the stairs together, he asked, "what do you think of Lynch's latest book?"

Alana told him, forcing herself not to think beyond the moment. Damian listened to her with rapt attention and, for that time, with the wind blowing in softly from the Atlantic, and the kiskadees twittering somewhere in the fading dusk, Alana found that she could pretend that they would be together like this always.

Eleven

The next month rolled by with alarming speed. It was almost as though nature were intent on cheating them both out of the precious time they had left together. Suddenly, it was April, the gennip trees were laden with soft sweet fruit, and Easter was just around the corner.

At school, the children were restless, and longing for the anticipated three-week break from studies and examinations. Alana found that she was just as impatient for classes to be over with, but for a completely different reason. She and Damian had planned to go across to Berbice during the Easter break and, though spending days and nights completely alone with him alarmed her, she coveted the time they had left together. She had told him that Harry would be away on a business trip, and that she wouldn't be missed. He had accepted her suggestion of an excursion into the hinterland of the country with as much eagerness as she had given it.

At home, she fabricated a story which she knew fooled no one, but which was a necessary ploy nonetheless. She had insisted that she go alone, unaccompanied by the ever-faithful Peters. There had been a gleam of understanding in her mother's eyes, and she had intervened and smoothed over the situation when her father would surely have objected.

* * *

On the morning before their intended departure, Alana received a piece of news that left her walking on air. It seemed impossible. Too good to be true. Divine providence; something. Lynch, her idol, her favorite author in the entire world, was going to make a stop in Guyana during his whirlwind book tour of South America and the Caribbean.

The thought that she might finally get to meet him filled her with exultation. The only thing that ruined her happiness was the knowledge that Damian could not know that Lynch would be in Guyana. Not yet, at any rate. The details of the author's stay were still being negotiated with the government, and Alana was under strict instruction to discuss the impending visit with no one. Lynch was apparently quite eccentric, guarding his privacy with a fierce dedication. Details of when he would arrive and where he would be staying were to be kept strictly hush-hush. But, eccentric or not, since celebrities hardly ever visited the country, Alana knew that Lynch would not be able to escape a ceremony or two, and would be expected to put in an appearance at the inevitable round of cocktail parties that would be given in his honor. Alana regretted that she could not share the news with Damian, because, although he was not a fan of the same magnitude as she, the news of Lynch's visit might have persuaded him to stay that much longer.

On the morning of Monday, April sixth, Alana was up and dressed before the last streaks of dawn were bleached from the sky by the rising sun. Her heart pounded with a mixture of anticipation and dread. As she carried her small suitcase down to the car, she popped into Harry's suite for a minute. As she had expected, he was already awake, despite the earliness of the hour.

He was propped up in bed, holding a large leather-bound legal text. He snapped it closed at her appearance, and glowered at her for a moment.

"Do you really think that this is the best thing to do? Going away with him?" She had told him of Damian's imminent departure, and had listened to his "I told you so's," with barely concealed irritation. She loved her brother, but sometimes his timing left much to be desired. She had expected sympathy and comfort from him. He had always been there for her in times of crisis, but now, when she needed his support the most, he withdrew it.

"Don't spoil this for me, Harry. Try to understand why I have to do it."

He fixed her with an unwavering stare. "And should you return with child, what do you intend to do then? Your Lothario will be on the other side of the Atlantic, probably getting some other naive girl into a similar mess."

Alana's hand tightened on the handle of her suitcase. "I've explained things to him. He won't try to get me into bed. He understands."

Harry grimaced. "Oh, he understands all right. He knows exactly how gullible you are." He stood up with a flourish. "There's something else he should understand, too—if he does anything at all to hurt you, by God, I'll hunt him down like the animal he is, and . . ."

"Harry," Alana interrupted, "I'm going." She could see that he was in the process of working himself into a fine temper. She pressed his hand. "He won't hurt me." Somehow, she knew that with a certainty.

"You'd better pray that he doesn't."

* * *

Alana arrived at Damian's cottage, and Peters gave her a lost-puppy-dog look.

"Sure you'll be okay?"

Alana nodded, and assured him she'd be fine. Anyone would think that she was six years old, instead of twenty-six. He wanted to carry her suitcase to the door, but she wouldn't let him. She waited for him to drive off, then she carried it there herself. Damian had prepared breakfast for them both: steaming jugs of hot chocolate, beef fritters, and breadfruit. He sat watching her as she ate. Usually he had a very hearty appetite but, this morning, he seemed preoccupied. Finally, he told her what was bothering him.

"If Harry doesn't care about you, why do you stay with him?"

Alana swallowed carefully, and the bitter irony of that question gave her lips a wry twist. What would he say if he knew that, just this morning, Harry had threatened his life, or would have, if she had let him.

"Harry and I have a very . . . special relationship. A marriage of convenience . . . of sorts."

He considered that for a moment, and Alana drank deeply from her jug so as to avoid the probing intensity of his eyes.

"The man's a fool." Damian swept his food into a dustbin. "We'd better get going."

The East Coast Highway was a long and winding stretch through coconut groves and wide rolling patches of unpopulated flatlands. The road curved perilously in places, then, just as suddenly, evened out to glide over bubbling creeks filled with hassa, a fish native to Guyana. The countryside was lush and green, unspoiled by progress; the air was fresh and sweet. It was possible to imagine that nothing existed outside of this peace and utter quiet. At one point, the road parted in respectful deference to the towering majesty of a huge purple heart tree. There was a bronze plaque affixed to the trunk. It was tarnished with age and, in places, the trunk of the tree had grown over the dull metal, obscuring the words embossed there. They stopped to take a closer look at it. The tree had stood there, in that exact spot, for at least a century. Its huge, scaly trunk and long, spindly arms had weathered the ravages of time with silent nobility, and Alana felt humbled in its presence.

As they approached Rosignol, the roadway became slightly less deserted. Cows ambled across in total disregard of the traffic, and farm workers walked along the grassy fringes, balancing huge sacks of rice on their shoulders. Damian was forced to brake hurriedly at one point when a small goat made a sudden dart from the side of the road and came to an abrupt halt directly before the car. It bleated pitiously and refused to budge, even when Damian honked the horn. Finally, Alana decided to get out and usher the frightened creature back across to safety. A ram on the other side of the road, attracted by the bright red of Alana's skirt, sidled up and took a yank at the fabric, almost dragging it right off of her. After a few frenzied seconds of tug of war, Alana managed to extricate herself from the clutches of the animal, and made a wild sprint back to the car with the goat in hot pursuit. She slammed the door, then peered out at the animal as it careened directly into the car with a soft thump.

"My God, it must be crazy."

She turned to see that Damian had collapsed against the steering wheel, weak with laughter. She punched him in the shoulder, and an unwilling smile tugged at her lips.

"It's really not that funny."

He gave another guffaw. "You didn't see yourself. I wish I'd had my camera out."

They drove on, and arrived at the lip of the Berbice River just after noon. The sun was bright and hot, and Alana rolled down the window and peered out. The Berbice River was the second largest in Guyana. It was so wide that, when you stood on one bank, it was impossible to see the other. The water was a muddy brown, deep and treacherous. Many an experienced swimmers had lost their lives in its depths. The surface of the water was calm, almost without a ripple, but, beneath, there lurked currents so strong that a grown man could be swept away to his death within seconds of falling into the water.

They had to wait in line for almost an hour before a ferry arrived, then another hour before they actually made it onto the barge. It seemed very unsafe to Alana, and she held her breath as Damian drove up the makeshift wooden plank that groaned and shuddered under the weight of the car. When they were finally aboard, Damian parked, and they both got out. From the leeward side of the vessel, there was nothing to be seen but wide stretches of shimmering brown water that foamed and curled around the sides of the ferry. When they cast off, Alana was barely aware of it. They just seemed to float along, skimming the water with a grace and elegance that was strangely incongruous for such an old and creaky vessel. Vendors walked about on board, selling everything from plantain chips and tamarind balls to roti, curry, and coconut water. Damian had some curry, even though Alana advised him not to eat it. He assured her with a grin, that he had a cast-iron stomach.

When they arrived in Berbice, it was early evening. The heat of the day had burnt off, leaving a refreshing breeze in its place. Alana had never visited this county, and she looked around with interest as they drove to the little guest house which her father's secretary had booked.

The guest house turned out to be a bit more than she had expected, and she saw the barely veiled surprise on Damian's face as they pulled off the road. The directions Alana had been given were excellent, and they had found the place with little difficulty. It was a rather official-looking three story residence, with a long line of well pruned palm trees standing on either side of the curving pink gravel driveway that led to the house. Alana felt a shard of cold panic clutch at her. Her father's secretary had made the arrangements for her; that meant that the people at the guest house would know who she was. She'd been so wrapped up in trying to convince her family that she should go to Berbice alone that she'd completely forgotten to tell the secretary not to let the guest-house staff know who she was.

"Damian," she spun in the seat to look at him, "let's go somewhere else."

He brought the car to a stop next to a cream Porsche, then turned to face her. He dropped a quick kiss on her lips.

"Don't worry," he said, "I can afford it."

He was out of the car and around to open her door before Alana could utter another word. What could she do? Maybe she could speak to the person in charge while Damian was unloading their suitcases. That just might work.

"Damian, I'll go ahead to sign in. I'll wait for you at the front desk."

He gave her a tolerant smile. "You're not embarrassed about this, are you? People do it every day." His eyebrows came together in a sudden frown. "We could sign in as a couple, if it would make you feel more comfortable?"

"No," Alana said, and she hoped he hadn't noticed that discordant squeak in her voice. "I'd much rather I went ahead first."

He lifted the cases from the trunk, and rested them beside him on the ground.

"I'll wait five minutes. Is that long enough?"

Alana nodded and hurried into the building. She was met immediately by a thin, efficient-looking woman in a starched blue tunic.

"Welcome," the woman beamed. "We've been expecting you. I am Mrs. Curten. I hope your trip over was pleasant?"

Alana assured her that it had been, then went into a hurried explanation of what she required. The proprietress was quite accommodating and, by the time Damian appeared, everything had been straightened out. The entire staff would be let in on the secret. She would not be treated in any way different from any other guest, and no mention would be made of her relationship to the Prime Minister.

Once they were in the suite, Alana breathed a relieved sigh. Damian rested the cases on the floor, and they both took a look around. The suite was nothing short of spectacular. It was done in shades of light mauve and pristine white. There were oriental throw rugs scattered on the floor in the sitting room, there was a breakfast nook complete with a microwave and stocked fridge, and there were two sprawling self-contained bedrooms, each equipped with its own black-marble Jacuzzi and sauna room. Sunlight filtered into the larger of the two bedrooms via a skylight which could be shaded by venetian blinds at the press of a button.

The beauty of it all robbed Alana of speech, and she wondered, then, whether Mrs. Curten had understood her request for nonpreferential treatment. Damian, too, appeared quite worried, and Alana could only assume that he was probably wondering at the cost of the entire ensemble.

Alana cleared her throat, and glanced at him for the first time.

"I had no idea they would give us anything this elaborate."

A smile tugged at the corners of Damian's lips. "I know."

Alana's brow furrowed in puzzlement. What did he mean by that?

"We could change to another one, if you don't like this?"

He stared at her for a long second. "What's important is, do you like it? I want you to be comfortable."

"Oh." Her eyes met his, and suddenly he was very close to her.

"Oh, what?" he said with a mock-serious lift to his brows. "Don't you know that, if you were mine, I'd spoil you rotten?" His arms stole around her, his fingers spanning her waist with ease.

"Would you do that?" she questioned, a note of teasing in her voice.

"I'd do that." He bent his head and nipped at her lips in a soft kiss. She pressed her lips to his, and he deepened the caress, his arms curving her into his body so that she felt the intimate throb of his groin. A shiver of excitement rippled through Alana, and she gave herself up to the sweet pleasure of his caresses, glorying in the feel of his skin so burningly close to hers. Much too soon, he withdrew his lips. Alana opened her eyes, and she found him looking at her, and she did not recognize the emotion in his eyes. It was new and bright and, in an instant, it was gone, to be replaced by the brooding sensuality that was always there.

"What are we going to do tonight?"

Alana was sure there was much more to that question than the words themselves suggested. There was a distinctly wicked glint in his eyes that caused her pulse to quicken.

"Unpack first . . ."

"Uhmm hmm." He pulled her to him again. "Go on."

"Then . . ."—she swallowed suddenly, making a strange croaking sound—"shower . . ." She was almost out of breath.

He kissed the side of her jaw. "Together?"

She pulled back. Harry was right; she might return with child if this onslaught kept up.

"No, we . . . we can't."

"Why can't we?" His mouth opened against her skin to pull the tender flesh on her neck within its warm cavern, and a raw shudder of pure feeling shook Alana.

"Damian . . ." Her voice was thick, trembling, uncontrolled.

"Lani, trust me," he murmured against her face.

His body was shaking, too, and Alana wished that she didn't have to resist him. But how would she explain away her obvious innocence, a "married" woman like herself? There was no explanation that would ring true, no man in the world who would believe that she was a married virgin. Damian would hate her. He would leave hating her. She didn't think she could live with that. She couldn't let him know that she had lied, that it had all been a lie.

A surge of desperation swept her, and she pulled roughly away from him.

"Damian, you promised me . . ." Her eyes were wild with panic.

"I'm breaking my promise. You've made me wait long enough. I can't stand much more of this." He approached her with a distinctly predatory gleam in his eyes. "Don't fight this, Lani. It's what we both want. Don't deny that you want me, too."

"I think we should take a bath," she said with pleading eyes.

He lifted her into his arms with a growl, "that's a start, anyway."

On the way to the bathroom in the master suite, he bent his head and kissed her into drugged compliance. He dispensed with his clothing quickly, stripping down to a pair of brief black elastic shorts that left little to the imagination.

Alana's eyes wandered his body in reluctant admiration—his broad muscular shoulders, hairy chest, hard whipchord stomach, and long sinewy legs. The body of an athlete, a beautiful brown Adonis. And he was looking at her in a way that stirred every hair follicle on her body.

Her clothes followed his and then she was standing before him clad in nothing more than her lacy bra and pink sweetheart underwear. Her heart beat like a trip hammer as he made a slow inspection of her generous curves.

His gaze lingered on the swell of her bosom, then dipped down to the plum-shaped birthmark just above her navel. He murmured something hoarse, then she was in his arms. He lifted her into the bubbling Jacuzzi, and the water lapped around them both. Alana started violently as a melodious peal of chimes echoed around the suite. They both were still for several seconds, neither able to decipher the origin of the sound. Then it came again.

"It's the front door," Alana whispered. "We'll have to get it."

Damian wrapped a thick robe about himself. "Stay where you are," he said to her. "I'll get rid of whoever it is."

He returned shortly afterwards, his face thunderous.

"There's a call for you in the manager's office. I tried to convince the bellhop to send it through here, but he keeps insisting that their phone system cannot accommodate transfers."

Alana stood, her expression worried. "Who was it?"

"He wouldn't say. I guess it's good old Harry, checking up on you."

Alana dressed rapidly, and Damian watched her in moody silence. She didn't look at him once while she slid into her clothes.

"Maybe we should go for dinner when I come back," she said. "I'm starving."

"So am I," he muttered, and Alana knew, without question, that he wasn't referring to food.

The phone call was from her father and, after assuring him that she was perfectly all right, she listened with mounting excitement to what he had to say. There was going to be a presentation of a special literary award to Lynch on the 24th of the month, and her father wondered whether she might like to do the honors. A decision had to be made that night: thus the reason for his call.

Alana assured him, with glowing eyes, that she'd love to do it. That meant that her vacation with Damian had to be cut short by a couple of days, but this was a once-in-a-lifetime chance, and she wouldn't miss it for the world.

When she returned to the suite, Damian was dressed in a cool sky-blue shirt and white slacks. His expression darkened at the sight of her face.

"I guess I don't need to ask who that was?"

Alana was about to deny his assumption, then realized that she couldn't very well tell him who had called. Her hesitation lengthened, and he turned away from her abruptly, but not before Alana glimpsed raw jealousy on his face.

"Let's go up to dinner."

The guest house was a curious mixture of the old and the ultramodern. Each meal was served on the top floor of the establishment, and all the patrons sat around one large dining table.

They walked up the curving lacquered staircase in silence. At the top of the stairs, Alana whispered, "Damian, you don't have to be upset with me."

He glanced at her, then away. "I'm not upset with you."

They were greeted by Mrs. Curten, and Alana prayed that the woman would remember not to inquire about her parents, or her brother Harry.

They were the only people in the dining room and, once they were seated and the proprietress had disappeared, Alana turned to Damian.

"There's no need to be jealous of Harry."

"Why not?" Damian turned unfathomable black eyes in her direction. He made no attempt to deny what she'd just said, much to Alana's surprise.

"Because . . . I don't love him that way."

His jaw tightened. "What way do you love him?"

Alana took a deep breath. "Like a brother?"

His eyebrows flicked together, forming a thick black pelt.

"The same way you feel about me, I guess?"

"No." And she was unable to say more, because Mrs. Curten appeared, carrying two steaming bowls of black-eyed pea soup. Damian rose to help her, and the woman beamed at him.

"Thank you, Mr. Collins, but I can manage." She placed the soup before them, then disappeared once more.

They lapsed into silence again, and Alana realized that she really was very hungry. The soup was thick and delicious, liberally sprinkled with small hard dumplings, peas, and succulent chunks of meat.

The main meal was metem, a traditional Guyanese dish with distinctive African influences. It was a sort of fish stew made with coconut milk and lots of ground vegetables like yams and edoes, and served with yellow plantains and huge fluffy sweet dumplings called duffs. Damian had never tasted metem before, and he savored the meal in the way a connoisseur might. He appeared to be rather open-minded about food, willing to eat whatever was served without the slightest hesitation. In fact, he appeared to view life as one big adventure, and seemed to be willing to open himself up to the myriad possibilities which came with having contact with different cultures.

After dinner, Mrs. Curten returned to inquire whether or not they would like dessert. But the meal had been so substantial that they both refused anything more. Alana caught sight of a bookcase which stood close to the windows, and she walked across to inspect it. She was acutely aware that Damian was watching her every movement. A soft breeze drifted into the room, stirring the wisps of hair which brushed against her face. She wanted to delay returning to the suite for as long as was possible without making him suspicious. Alana chose a novel at random, and sat in a high-backed chair. Damian came to stand by the window and, for several minutes, he said nothing. His face was completely devoid of emotion as he stared out at the approaching darkness. Alana glanced up at him, and he seemed to sense her movement, and turned.

"You're afraid of me." His voice was hard and gritty, and held a trace of hurt.

Alana's fingers played with the edge of a page, bending it back and forth until a crease appeared. She wasn't afraid of him; she was afraid of losing him, but that seemed inevitable, whatever she chose to do.

"I can't view an intimate relationship in the casual way you do, Damian. If you can't understand that, you'll never understand me."

"Let's go down." He looked suddenly tired, and it was as though he'd completely lost interest in their discussion.

At the door to the second bedroom, he said goodnight, then disappeared into the master room without giving her his usual goodnight kiss.

Alana took a quick shower, then hung her clothes in the walk-in closet. Sachets of potpourri had been provided, and she hung one on each hanger, listening all the while for sounds in the next room. She wondered if they would ever fully understand each other. They were so different, coming from two totally different worlds, almost. His was free and easy and, apparently, anything was permissible. Hers was bound by duty and a strict code of ethics. They appeared to be incompatible on every level except the obvious. Maybe Harry had been right. Maybe she should look for someone who viewed life in the same way she did, someone from their circle of friends, someone Guyanese. She pounded her pillow in frustration. Why did life have to be so complicated? She wanted Damian, not someone else, and it didn't matter one iota whether he was from Mars, or sold shoes on a street corner for a living.

Shortly after midnight, rain began to fall in heavy torrents, and Alana got up to close the windows. Loud claps of thunder crashed outside, and the sky lit up in occasional bursts of jagged light. A sudden knock on the door coincided with a clap of thunder, and Alana jumped, despite herself.

"Damian?"

He answered from the other side, and she pulled open the door. He was still fully dressed, and she looked at him with immediate concern.

"Is something wrong?"

He shrugged. "I wasn't in bed yet. I wondered if you were okay."

She leaned on the doorjamb. "I'm okay, how about you?"

He shoved his hands into his pockets. "I couldn't sleep. Can I come in?"

She stepped backward, and he entered and stood just inside, looking a bit uncomfortable.

"I want to stay . . . with you."

Alana cleared her throat, and he hurried on. "I spent the last couple of hours thinking, and I want you to know that I'm trying to understand how you feel. It's not easy for me. I've never denied myself before, never wanted to. But, for you, I'll try." He held out a hand, and she placed hers in his.

She whispered, "I'll try, too."

Their eyes met, and she saw a flicker of raw and untamed emotion that burnt brightly then was quickly suppressed.

A few minutes later, he lay next to her in bed. Her head rested on his chest, and his arms were wrapped around her, making her feel snug and warm. She wasn't sure when it was, but sometime between listening to the patter of raindrops and counting Damian's heartbeats, she fell asleep.

Twelve

The next few days passed in an idyllic haze. They spent many hours exploring the countryside. Berbice was a peculiar mixture of town and country, a sweeping panorama of little shops nestled amongst open-air markets and movie houses. There was an Old-World charm to it all, and Alana was thrilled that Damian enjoyed the quaint beauty of her country so much. He took along a little notepad and, much to Alana's delight, took copious notes on everything he saw.

Just outside New Amsterdam, they stopped to have a look at the farmers as they worked in the fields. There were vast swamplands filled with thick shoots of sugar cane, and rolling hills thick and green with weedy stalks of rice. Life here was raw and vital, at times harsh, but always fresh and unspoiled. There was a certain charm to seeing brown rice paddies being dried along the roadside on huge brown sacks, and there was an unwritten understanding that the rice had the right of way. All traffic went to great pains to avoid the sacks, even when at times they stretched almost to the center of the road. The farmers were most accommodating to interested passersby as vehicle after vehicle pulled over to watch with interest as the paddy was turned with large paddles. Damian even bent and trailed his hand in the hot paddy, and a grinning farmer encouraged him to take a handful. The shells were slick and hard, protecting the white kernels of rice from the hot noon-day sun.

A mile or two down from the drying paddy were more cane fields that were nothing more than dried-up stumps amidst blackened expanses of earth. This cane, Alana explained to Damian, was just about to be sent to the sugar factory. The fields had been burnt to get rid of snakes and, more importantly, to concentrate the sucrose content of the cane and make it easier to extract. She gave him a quick summary of how that process occurred chemically, and he wrote that down on his notepad too. She was pleased to discover that he had no hangups about learning something from her. There were some men, she knew, who would rather pretend a knowledge which they did not possess than admit that they didn't know it all. It took a strong sense of security in oneself, and Damian, she was learning more and more, was a very secure man

By the end of the week, they had explored most of the areas surrounding Rosignol. They had stopped at a sugar-cane factory and watched as the cut cane was unloaded from the pontoons which traversed the huge sweet-water trenches. Damian had wanted to go in for a tour, but Alana had managed to talk him out of that. There would surely have been people in management positions in the factory who would've recognized her.

On Easter Sunday, they went to church. They slid into the back pew in an old whitewashed building. It looked more like an abandoned schoolhouse than a church, but Alana thoroughly enjoyed the little service. Damian held her hand throughout the proceedings, and sang lustily off-key from an old hymn book. People around him nodded approvingly, Amened, and looked quite solemn as he hit a particularly sour note.

Later, they went shopping for kites. The next day was Easter Monday, another national holiday in Guyana. Everyone took to the streets to fly kites. Ofttimes, it was almost impossible to see even a patch of blue sky. There were kites of every size, shape, and color. It signified the ascendance of Christ, and it was a glorious spectacle, and also a lot of fun.

They decided to go to the open-air market. Alana knew from experience that the best kites were always found there. Damian chose a huge multi-colored diamond-shaped kite with an aggressive snarl painted onto the face. A competing vendor sucked his teeth in disgust at Damian's choice.

"The k-yite," he said, drawing out the syllable in typical Guyanese fashion, "gon' bus' way. D'tail en lang e'nuff."

Damian looked at the shorter man in utter incomprehension. Alana whispered to him with a giggle, "He said the kite's going to burst away from you because the tail isn't long enough."

Damian inspected his purchase. "It looks pretty well balanced to me. He's just trying to hustle me for a sale."

The vendor tugged at Alana's hand. "Come beytah, I gat one nice k-yite fuh yuh."

He presented Alana with a four-foot masterpiece of green, black, and gold. The tail was a long curve of rope with small scraps of cloth tied to it at intervals. He attached a giant roll of twine, which he called a "balla," to the face, and stood back with a triumphant grin. Alana had never flown a kite before. Many times, she had watched them soar like giant butterflies, and had wished that she might join in the fun, but it had never been possible. Now she stood staring at the beauty in her hands, with a mixture of excitement and uncertainty. Was this the right one? Would this be the one to glide above the rest, and not plummet to the ground, becoming a tangled and broken wreck?

"What do you think?" she asked Damian.

"It's certainly colorful," he said, with a wry twist of his lips.

"Dat is d'best k-yite hey," the vendor said with a nod of encouragement.

"Okay. I'll take this one." Suddenly Alana felt stupidly happy, and free, and she smiled up at Damian. His eyes glinted down at her, tolerant and amused.

"Such little things make you happy, my sweet girl."

Alana squeezed his hand. How could she fully express that when she was with him, everything made her happy?

The next day, Mrs. Curten packed them a large picnic basket and, in the freshness of the morning sun, they set off. Sixty-three Beach was a kite-flier's mecca, and they headed there. It was the best wide-open space to be found for miles, the perfect place to laze, have a dip in the ocean, and fly the kites. When they arrived, there were already quite a few families sprinkled at various points along the long stretch of silt-brown sand. The tradition at Sixty-three Beach was that you drove your vehicle directly onto the sand, then camped wherever you stopped. Damian chose the shady cover of two enormous coconut trees. He helped Alana spread their towels on the sand, then he brought out the kites, careful not to puncture the delicate paper that was stretched across the frames. There were children running excitedly up and down the beach with half-airborne kites trailing behind them. The beach was beginning to fill up quickly, and, already, several kites dotted the sky. It wasn't really hot yet. A soft breeze blew in from the glittering expanse of brown water and, as Alana sat tightening the strings on her kite, the wind pulled at the singer at the bottom, making it buzz madly.

Damian was dressed in shorts and a muscle vest, and he sat beside her as he finished hitching up his kite. Alana looked at him as he worked. They had slept together in the same bed, shared the same living space for the past week, and he had made no attempts to push things further. He was exercising remarkable restraint, and Alana couldn't help wondering why. He looked up suddenly, and caught her watching him. That slow, familiar smile that she knew so well curved his lips, and Alana returned it, feeling her heart turn over in her chest. He leaned across and pressed a quick kiss to her mouth.

"Do you want to take a quick dip first?"

"Okay."

They disrobed, and Alana felt her eyes drawn to the broad strength of his shoulders, the hard flatness of his stomach, and the long stretch of hair-sprinkled brown legs. He was watching her, too, and, strangely enough, she liked his eyes on her, liked the way they ran over her scanty green bikini, pausing at the deep scoop in the front.

A frown rippled his forehead for a minute, and he bent to retrieve the vest he had just discarded. "Maybe you'd better wear this over the top, it's too . . ."

Alana grinned at him, enjoying his discomfort. "Damian, you're a prude. I never would have expected it of you."

He glowered at her. "You have no idea how appealing you are. I don't want to have to fight off a slobbering pack of men."

Alana looked around. "I don't see any slobbering packs. No one's even paying any attention to us."

"Yet," he said with a deepening scowl. "Just humor me, please."

Alana took the vest, and slid it over her head. It smelled like warmth, cologne, and Damian. When she was finished, she did a little pirouette. "Satisfied?"

He gave her a considering stare. "Maybe you should wear my pants, too."

"Absolutely not," Alana said with a giggle, and she took off across the sand toward the water. Damian pounded behind her, and she splashed into the water and waded out to waist level. The water was cool and refreshing against her skin, and she scooped up a handful to examine it. It was as clear as spring water, but as soon as it trickled back to the sea, it once again merged with the all-pervading brown. Damian came up behind her, and for the next fifteen or so minutes they engaged in a madcap game of water tag, splashing and frolicking in the water like two young seals.

Finally, Alana called a halt to their game by tearing from the water and flopping exhausted onto one of the big towels beneath the coconut palms. Damian stayed for a while longer, then he, too, emerged. Alana dried him off with a soft white towel, and he watched her, without comment through eyes that were glittering and intensely black. When she was finished, she glazed his torso with baby oil. He appeared to enjoy the gentle touch of her hands and, when she stopped, he tipped back his head and said, "You can't be finished yet."

She pinched his earlobe. "It's time to get those kites in the air."

"All in good time." He reached for the bottle of oil. "You're next."

The rest of the day passed in a blur of laughter. Damian's kite soared proudly into the sky with little effort, stayed aloft for exactly two seconds, then plunged without warning into a coconut tree. A family of boisterous children who happened to be old pros at handling kites suggested, quite helpfully, that Damian climb the vertical coconut-tree trunk and retrieve the kite. When he declined, the youngest member of the group, a spritely boy who couldn't have been much more than twelve years old, clambered up the tree with ease and hefted the huge kite from the branches. It was undamaged, by some stroke of luck, and the boy, yelling instructions to Damian below, held it out to the wind. Damian took off down the beach in response to encouraging yells, with the kite trailing behind him like a drunken bat. Alana watched as the kite made a determined effort to rise, then plunged with abandon into the sea. This time, there was no saving it.

Alana ran up to Damian, chortling heartily. His camera swung from around her neck, and a radiant flush lit her face.

"That was terrible," she said. "The worst performance I've seen here today."

He turned with a grin. "Oh, really? Well, let's see how you do." He grabbed her hand, and they jogged up the beach to where her kite still rested. The beach was packed with people, and the sky was a glorious splash of color. The sun seemed much hotter here at the beach, but hardly anyone noticed. Alana's kite climbed into the sky easily, and she unraveled her ball of twine, letting it soar higher still. The wind picked up, making the kite buzz loudly, and causing the twine to bite painfully into Alana's hands. Damian stood behind her and helped her hold the dancing kite steady. It wasn't an easy job, trying to keep it from becoming tangled in the twine of other kites. Some people attached razor blades to the tails of their kites just to avoid this even-

tuality. Any wayward kite that came too close would be
cut loose by the sharp blades.

After an hour of battling the wind and staring almost
directly into the bright sun, they tied the kite to a stump
in the ground and settled down to the picnic lunch
Mrs. Curten had packed. She had provided a wide selection of crackers, cheese sandwiches made the Guyanese way, fried chicken and tennis rolls, and curry and
roti. She had also packed a container of ginger beer,
one of Mauby, and several bottles of cream soda, Alana's
favorite. There was so much food that Damian invited
the children who had helped him in his unsuccessful
kite-flying attempt to join them.

They sat eating for quite a while, and the conversation
drifted to Guyanese folklore. The boy, Mark, who had
ousted the kite from the coconut tree, started the session of story swapping with an apparently innocent
comment. He was of the opinion that, at nightfall, a
famed man-creature called the Masacurra man rose
from the depths of the sea and spirited away little children who were still out flying their kites on the beach.
This prompted an immediate outburst of disbelief, and
an almost tangible undercurrent of fear from the rest
of the brood. They all looked to Damian for confirma-
tion, and in the spirit of things, he went along with the
young boy. Not to be outdone, another boy in the group
raised his right arm and displayed proudly the band of
black rubber which encircled his wrist. He had gone to
an Obeah man, he said, looking threateningly at the
young boy, Mark, and this ring of rubber could ward
off Masacurra men, Bacoo, and everything else the un-
derworld had to offer. Mark, however, refused to accept
defeat, and with an eloquence and flow that belied his
twelve years, he plunged the gathering into a ball of

suspense as he told of Old Hige, which sucked the blood from young infants, and pretty young women called Lajabless. These young beauties could run as fast as a horse, and justifiably so, since they were equipped with one human leg, and one goat leg. Once they made eye contact with a poor unsuspecting man, his soul was lost forever. At that point in the story, Damian lifted the vest which Alana was wearing, and peered with interest at her legs.

"Just checking," he said with a solemn expression, and the children burst into relieved laughter.

Later, Damian and Alana took turns at flying the kite, and then, when evening began to fall, they repacked the picnic basket and prepared to go. Everyone else was beginning to do the same, and the sky seemed suddenly forlorn and empty. Most of the children had disappeared, but the boy called Mark was still flying his kite, paying little attention to the approaching darkness. His face was set in lines of concentration as he guided his kite through the sky, letting it swoop and twirl, then holding it steady once again.

"You do that very well." Damian said, walking up.

Mark shrugged. "Uhmm hmm."

"Ever thought of becoming a writer?" Damian asked.

The boy shrugged again. "You mean like V.S. Naipaul and Edgar Mittelholzer?"

Damian recognized the two men the boy mentioned. They were both distinguished West Indian writers.

"Those are great writers."

Mark turned and gave Damian a questioning look. "Yuh really think I'd make a good writer like them?"

Damian nodded. "You certainly have a good imagination, and there's a definite rhythm to your storytelling. Why don't you think about it?"

Mark grinned. "I've already got a couple of stories. Never shown anyone though."

Damian pulled out his notepad and asked the boy for his address. After a moment's hesitation, Mark gave it to him.

"I'll write to you," Damian said, "and you can send me some of your stories so I can look them over. Agreed?"

The boy nodded. "Thanks, man."

In the car on the way back, Alana watched the pink of the approaching sunset. She had heard the exchange between Damian and the little boy.

"That was a really nice thing you did for Mark," she said.

Damian swerved to avoid a hole in the road. "I don't claim to be a literary expert, but I'm sure that little tyke has some talent."

"You might be right," Alana agreed. "He did seem to be quite bright."

"Uhmm." Damian pressed her hand. "Did you have fun today?"

"It was the best," Alana said, with a dreamy expression on her face. "Thank you." She pressed a kiss to the side of his face, and she felt the muscles in his cheek pull beneath her lips.

"You would do that when I'm driving." He gave her a quick look. "You look tired."

"Oh, not really. You must be, though, from all this driving, and running up and down the beach."

Damian smiled. "I'm not exactly a decrepit old man, you know."

"I know," she said, throwing him a wicked glance.

"You'd better behave yourself, young lady. You can

dish it out, but you know that you can't take it once I get interested."

"A very devious psychological ploy," Alana responded. "But I'm a little too wise to fall for that one."

Damian grinned, and they rode the rest of the way home in companionable silence. When they got to the suite, there was a jug of wine, a thick loaf of warm bread, and a hunk of flaky cheese waiting for them under a huge silver dome in the breakfast nook. There was also a note there, and Damian picked it up and read it quickly.

"Are you going to want dinner later tonight?"

Alana grimaced. "Not after all we ate today, plus this." She motioned to the silver dome.

"Okay. I'll ring up and let Mrs. Curten know while you're in the bath."

Alana took a leisurely shower. The straps of her bikini had printed out on her skin, and the darker areas of flesh were sore and quite tender. She washed her hair, too. There were twigs, sand, and other bits of debris tangled in the thick black tresses, and it took a bit of doing to get her hair clean. She heard Damian moving around somewhere outside as she emerged from the glass cubicle. She slipped into a thick terry bathrobe, and winced with discomfort as the rough fabric grazed against her skin. She dried her hair first, combing through the tangles until her hair was smooth and soft, then she slipped into fresh undies. When she emerged, Damian was seated on the bed. He had already bathed and changed. His expression was enigmatic, and he watched her as she walked to the closet to get her clothes.

"Are you sunburnt?"

"A little." It was actually a lot. Her skin was suddenly stinging very badly.

"Let me see." His hands peeled back the collar of the bathrobe, and Alana flinched as his fingers probed a sensitive spot on her shoulder.

"Take off the robe and lie on the bed; I have something that might help."

She met his eyes, and he smiled at her. There was nothing there but concern. She stepped out of the robe, and lay facedown on the bed. He sat beside her a few minutes later, and she closed her eyes as his strong fingers massaged cold, soothing Noxema into her pained flesh. He seemed to know exactly where the sore spots were, and his fingers skimmed across her skin like magic. After a while, he asked her to turn over, and she did so without hesitation. She was facing him now, and her eyes opened to watch him as he leaned over her, intent on his task. Her skin was tingling now, but it wasn't because of the sunburn—that pain had all but faded.

When his fingers stilled, she felt cheated, and her hand lifted to urge his into motion again. His fingers moved in response, but, this time, there was a completely different quality to his touch. He was almost lying over her, and Alana knew that she should stop him, but her hands were rising to touch his sleek shoulders, stealing into the neckline of his shirt, exploring the hard, warm skin. His body froze, as though he were afraid that any movement on his part might distract her, make her realize what it was she was doing.

He bent his head, and their lips met, and clung. He held her gently, whispering her name as he pressed kisses to her face, neck, and arms. He was murmuring something which Alana couldn't quite make out. She was caught in a tide of emotion so strong that, even if she had wanted to stop him, she wouldn't have had the willpower to do so. But she didn't want him to stop, she realized. She wanted him to go on, and on, until they reached the natural conclusion, the one both their bodies craved, the one that would keep her warm on rainy nights when he was gone.

She murmured something about contraception, and he gave her a reassuring kiss. He was gone from her for just a minute. When he returned, she held him close with trembling fingers, and helped him get rid of the flimsy barriers separating them. His heart pounded against hers, and she touched his face with loving hands.

"Damian." It was an entreaty, a caress, and he groaned her name in response.

He made love to her with a slow intensity, first soft and sweet, then uncontrollably hard and passionate. She clung to him, eyes closed, not caring what came afterward, just content to know that she was holding the only man she loved, would ever love, in her arms. He groaned her name, his fingers tangling in her hair. It was as though he couldn't get enough of her; couldn't touch her enough, couldn't kiss her enough. His breath mingled with hers, and Alana knew that this sharing was worth the pain that would surely come.

They fell asleep together, her head tumbled against his chest, his arms holding her as if he expected her to escape from him during the night. He made love to her again in the depth of the night, his voice husky and encouraging, and then again just before dawn. She awoke to find him watching her. He was propped up on one elbow, wide awake, and his lips curved into the kind of smile that only lovers can share.

"Good morning."

Alana felt her face flush with heat, and she returned his greeting shyly. She wondered when he would begin questioning her, and what she would say. He must have known that this had been her first time. He bent over and kissed her, his lips warm and firm.

"Stacy called. Something's come up. I have to return to Georgetown at the end of the week."

"Oh." Alana sat up and pulled the covers up under her arms. A thousand thoughts rushed through her head. Was he leaving because she had been a virgin, and he was sickened by her for having lied to him? Or was it because the thrill of the chase was now over, and he no longer found her interesting?

He seemed not to notice her distress as he climbed out of bed and slid into a robe. Shame, deep and dark, ran through her, and then anger—more at herself than at him. She had allowed him to treat her in this way. He must have known that she had been innocent, yet he had said nothing. Not even a passing query as to how she might be feeling the morning after. Not a question about Harry, and what this all meant. He had just wanted to bed her, and nothing else. How dare he kiss her as though he cared about her? How could he make her feel happy, when it was all a lie? A foolish, disgusting lie. Maybe he didn't even know that she'd been a virgin. He was just as Harry had said. A roaming, rutting Lothario.

"I'll shower first this morning. Okay?" He gave her a warm smile, and Alana forced her lips to respond. She wouldn't give him the satisfaction of knowing that he had the ability to hurt her so deeply.

"Fine." She wouldn't be there when he got out of the shower. She stared at the back of his head as he disappeared into the bathroom and shut the door. She made up her mind in that instant. She wouldn't see him again. This was it, the end of the affair that never was. The end of the joke. Damian Collins would never be allowed to hurt her again. She would leave her clothes, and have them picked up later. Scribble him a note explaining that she wouldn't be seeing him again. And, if she hurried, she could be on a twin engine to Georgetown in an hour, and out of his life for good.

She heard him in the bathroom singing loudly off-key, the shower going, and tears misted her vision. She wasn't strong enough to say goodbye to him. This way was much better.

Thirteen

Alana spent the rest of the week holed up in her suite at home. Harry had not questioned her about her premature return and, about that, she was grateful. She had cried herself dry of tears, and many times she had found herself on the verge of ringing the cottage in Llamaha Gardens to see whether Damian had gotten back yet. She wouldn't speak, wouldn't let him know who was on the other end, she just wanted to hear his voice again. But every time she reached for the phone, she stopped herself. Damian would know that it was her. His number was unlisted. So, she spent her time reading Lynch, and trying to forget that she loved Damian Collins, forcing herself to remember that he didn't love her. She was almost through the thick book which Damian had given her. The novel provided some escape, and she found herself retreating more and more into the world which the talented author created with such flowing ease. The tiny bright spot in an otherwise lackluster existence was the thought that she would be presenting a special literary award to Lynch himself in a few days. She had always wanted to meet the man, and she had convinced her father to invite the author back to the house for dinner after the award ceremony. She had loaned Harry a couple of Lynch's works, and he, who normally read nothing but law

books, had to comment with grudging admiration that
the novels were, in fact, topnotch and, without a doubt,
deserving of the award.

On Friday, the house was a buzz of activity. The formal
dining room, which was hardly ever used unless a visiting dignitary was coming to dinner, had been aired and
the furniture dusted and new drapes hung. A special
chef had been brought in to prepare dinner, and her
father's best liqueurs were brought out. Harry came in
early from court, and set out a collection of his favorite
law tomes. A man like Lynch, he told Alana with a grin,
was bound to appreciate such good, solid writing. Personally, Alana found Harry's law books extremely bor-
ing, and felt that Lynch might be of the same mind,
but she hadn't the heart to burst her brother's bubble.
Even her mother, a very level-headed woman who had
greeted visiting sheiks and kings alike with the same
unshakable aplomb, got swept up in the excitement,
and went out and got herself a new sleek haircut in
honor of the occasion.

That evening, Alana dressed with especial care. An
elegant linen dress, a dash of perfume, her hair swept
up into a smooth chignon. She had to admit, she did
look the part: svelte, beautiful, in control. Her face gave
no indication of the turmoil that lay behind the cool
smile and steady eyes. This was her first official function
since her return from Britain and, before she left the
house, she was given a quick briefing on protocol.
Lynch was apparently a highly antisocial character who
rarely attended public events. He also appeared to shun
physical contact, so Alana was instructed to shake his

hand and present the award without the usual obligatory peck on the cheek.

They arrived at the Cultural Center in the official manner. The large black State car with the Guyanese flag flying from posts on either side of the hood, a police escort with sirens blaring. Her mother was seated across from her in the huge car, and Harry sat by a window. Alana found that she was more than a little nervous. It wasn't every day that one got to meet the great Lynch. Peculiar eccentricities aside, the man was a literary giant, and it was a distinct honor for her to be in the same room as he.

Harry squeezed her hand as they climbed from the car. This was a big event, and newspaper photographers jostled for pictures. They posed for a few, then hurried into the building amidst flashing bulbs. They were greeted by Mr. Reuben, a rather artistic-looking little man with gentle eyes and nervous gestures. He had organized the event, and he seated them personally, up front near the stage. The auditorium was filled with people, and Alana turned her head surreptitiously to scour the faces of those seated along the front row. She nodded, smiling, as people recognized her.

"I wonder which one he is?" she whispered to Harry.

Her brother turned his head and gave a quick look.

"Probably that silver-haired man over there. He looks distinguished enough, and he's in the right age bracket."

Alana's heart leapt as she exchanged a smile with the man Harry had indicated. "Isn't it peculiar that we shouldn't know what he looks like?"

Harry shrugged. "Creative people tend to be peculiar." He seemed to consider that statement explanation enough, and Alana turned to look at the elderly man again, and froze as she saw Damian enter the auditorium. Big and tall and so handsome. He looked like a carefully groomed tiger. He was elegant in a trim, tailored suit. His face appeared slightly thinner, though Alana realized that that could have been just an illusion fostered by the subdued lighting. Her heart pounded in her chest as he came closer, and she ducked her head behind Harry so that he wouldn't see her. Of all places, why had he chosen to come to this function, tonight? More importantly, how had he gotten in? It was strictly by invitation only. Her eyes stole across the rows to where he was seated. He was right next to the silver-haired man. Next to Lynch. There was no way that she could get out of this now. She had to go ahead and present the award. Not that it really mattered any longer whether he knew who she was.

The first strains of the national anthem rang out, and everyone rose to their feet. The program was beginning. There would be a musical segment, a short skit based on one of Lynch's works, then the presentation of the award. As they sat once again, and the lights dimmed completely, Alana found that her eyes kept stealing around to take a peek at Damian. She could barely make out his face in the darkness, but she could see that he had his chin propped on his fingertips. He had arrived without a female companion, and Alana felt a deep sense of relief at that. At least he hadn't replaced her yet.

The program was very lively and entertaining, but Alana found that she was hardly listening to what was going on. Quite a few times, Harry gave her a little prod, and she saw her mother cast a worried eye in her direction. By the time the award segment arrived, she was as taut as the string of a bow, and she found that she couldn't remember the short speech which she had rehearsed. Had she planned to thank Lynch for visiting Guyana, present him with the award, then quote a passage from his latest book? Had it been the other way around? Or had she intended any of that at all? She couldn't, for the life of her remember.

There was a tense readiness in the crowd as Mr. Reuben moved to the podium and gave Lynch a short introduction. There was an immediate outburst of cheering, and everyone rose to their feet. Alana's knees wobbled dangerously, and Harry gripped her arm in concern.

"Lani, are you all right?" he whispered in a fierce undertone. She nodded. She wanted to get this over with; the waiting was killing her. Her stomach fluttered uncomfortably; the crowd remained on its feet, cheering. A man was making his way to the stage, and everyone's eyes were on him. But something was wrong, something was horribly wrong, and Alana's tongue cleaved to the roof of her mouth as time seemed to unravel in slow motion. Harry hadn't recognized him yet, but as soon as he sprang up the stairs and stepped into the floodlights, she heard her brother's harsh intake of breath. Damian.

Alana sat back down, hard, her hand pressed to her mouth. Her fevered brain refused to accept it. Maybe there was some other reason why Damian was standing before the microphone and waiting for the applause to die down. Maybe the old man next to him had fallen ill suddenly, and he was up there about to explain what had happened. He just couldn't be D.C. Lynch. It wasn't possible. She knew Lynch, and he wasn't Damian. She could hear Harry grinding his teeth next to her, and caught the starry-eyed expression in her mother's eyes before she could wipe it away. Alana felt frozen, totally numbed, when he began to speak. He smiled and said a few words of thanks. Then Mr. Reuben was introducing her, saying her name, but her feet were solid clumps of ice. She couldn't move, surely. But everyone was cheering again and, somehow, she rose and made it up the short flight of steps into the spotlight. Damian turned toward her, and he met her eyes, but there was no expression in them, no warmth, no recognition.

Under the heat of the spotlight, she began to come back to life; part of the shock had ebbed. Her prepared speech came back, and she thanked him in a stiff and composed voice, her brain churning all the while. He had lied to her. Had led her on, listening to her ramble for hours about how great Lynch was. All the while laughing secretly at her stupidity. Small wonder that he never spoke about what he did for a living, always clamming up whenever she probed a little. And all the while she had been feeling guilty about not telling him that she wasn't really married. He'd probably known all along. He hadn't even appeared surprised that Alana Britton, the girl he had spent the last few months with, was the Prime Minister's daughter, free, unencumbered, and definitely not married. He had made a fool of her, but he wouldn't be allowed to again. Never again.

She shook his hand, and his fingers tightened on hers for a minute. Her mother was beaming with pride from the audience. Alana passed on the statuette of a man frozen in bronze, bent forever over a sloping pile of books. Damian accepted it and, from the corner of her eye, Alana could see Mr. Reuben in the wings offstage, motioning to her to keep her distance from the author. Alana felt her lips curl with the bitter irony of it all. Yes, D.C. Lynch was eccentric. She remembered very well that she wasn't supposed to place her lips on his cheek, but no one had said anything about her palm. She heard the horrified collective gasp of a hundred or so people as her hand connected with Damian's smiling face, and she was vaguely aware of the thud that Mr.

Reuben made as he slumped, unconscious, to the floor. But her triumph was short-lived, as she was dragged into Damian's powerful embrace and subjected to a punishing, and very prolonged, kiss. He released her amidst popping camera bulbs and said, in steely tones, "Time for dinner, I think."

Two men Alana recognized as bodyguards were visibly restraining Harry. And her mother, who seemed the least affected by what had just occurred, appeared to be giving her brother a good talking-to.

How they got out of the crowded auditorium, Alana would never know. Harry and her mother rode back to the house in one car, and Alana and Damian in another. As the big car skimmed along the streets, the full enormity of what she had let happen began to hit her in steady, unrelenting waves. The repercussions would be disastrous. Front-page pictures in the newspaper of her slapping D.C. Lynch, juxtaposed with those of her clinched in the author's arms in what could only be interpreted as an embrace of passion . . . only *she* would know better. Calls for a public apology. The literary world would be up in arms, defending one of its own. Such a public slight would not be tolerated. The reputation of the country would be put on the line. Thousands, maybe millions, of dollars could be lost because of her. And her father: her father would have a fit. A royal fit.

Both cars arrived at once, one behind the other, and Alana dreaded the scene which she knew awaited her as soon as they were all behind closed doors. She hadn't spoken a word to Damian, or he to her, for the entire journey, and now she flinched away from him as he attempted to help her from the car. Harry and her mother disappeared into the house, and Alana quickened her footsteps. Damian's hand shot out to restrain her.

"Aren't you forgetting your manners, Miss Britton?" And Alana was very aware that he went to considerable pains to emphasize the "Miss."

"Oh, shut up," she barked at him, and earned a baffling grin.

Her father was waiting for them as they entered the formal sitting room, and Alana recognized the expression on his face. She hadn't seen it in years, not since she had tied the Ambassador of England's son to the malaka tree at their house in Linden and scared him to death with tales of the Masacurra man. Harry was standing by a window looking out, and Alana could see the spasmodic clenching of his jaw as he attempted to control his temper. Her mother was seated in a chair in the far corner of the room, looking surprisingly pleased with herself.

"Mr. Lynch." Her father gave Damian's hand a hearty shake. "Let me introduce my wife, Eugenia, my son, Harry, and of course you've already met my daughter . . . Alana."

Her mother nodded, smiling. Harry muttered something barely civil, and spun around again to glare out the window.

"Glad to finally meet you, sir, and, please, call me Damian." He returned her father's handshake, and managed to look as though he was presented with situations such as these everyday.

When she and Damian had seated themselves, her father walked across to where a little bar had been set up.

"Can I offer anyone a liqueur? Irish creme, Damian?" Alana sensed that an explosion of some sort was somewhere in the offing. She wasn't fooled for a minute by her father's dulcet tones.

Damian accepted the drink, but Alana felt that she had no stomach for the sweet, creamy liqueur. She felt a wild urge to get up and flee from the room—the tension was eating at her nerves, taking huge bites at a time.

Her father returned to sit opposite Damian. His face was emotionless, almost serene. A bad sign. It usually meant that he'd come to some astronomical decision, one from which he would refuse to be swayed. Alana speculated wildly. Maybe her father was going to promise Damian that, in return for his public humiliation, he would disown his daughter . . . cut her from his will . . . throw her out of the house . . .

"I hope you will accept my sincere apologies for this evening's misconduct, Damian. My daughter, of course, will issue a public statement apologizing for any inconvenience which her actions may have caused you."

"Thank you, sir, but I'm afraid that will not be sufficient."

Alana gasped with outrage. She was being humiliated before her family, in his presence, plus she was to suffer future embarrassment in public, and that was not enough for the swine. She should have slapped him twice, and much harder than she did; at least the memory of that would take her through the ordeal that lay ahead.

"I understand that you've been through a lot Damian, but I'm sure that if we think this thing out calmly, we can come to terms. Tell me, what would you suggest?"

Alana turned glittering eyes in his direction, willing him to suggest some greater humiliation for her to withstand. He gave her an arrogant smile, and she had to restrain herself from slapping him again.

"I'm afraid to say that nothing short of marriage to

your daughter will salvage the damage she has done to my reputation."

Alana felt the blood leave her head, and the room faded to black for half a second. She couldn't have heard him correctly. She just couldn't have. A stunned silence had fallen across the room and, in the tense waiting, Alana saw red. Of all the bleeding nerve. The damnable conceit of the man. Marry him? If he were the last male on the planet, she would never look twice in his direction. How dare he make such a suggestion? She rose to her feet, quivering with rage, "I will not marry him."

Harry shot her a look of open admiration. "I think you'd better rethink that last request, Collins," Harry said, coming to stand next to Alana and wrapping a muscled arm around her waist. He was itching for a confrontation with Damian—it was in his stance, and the challenge sparkled in his eyes. Damian gave him a cold stare, then turned toward Alana's confused father, who, for the first time in his life, appeared to be at a total loss for words.

"Could I have a minute alone with Alana?"

"Harry stays," Alana bit out, and her brother grinned defiantly at Damian.

Her mother, who had been observing the proceedings without comment thus far, suddenly took charge of the situation and ordered her husband and son from the room.

"I'll be back if you need me." Harry mouthed to Alana, and she gave him a grateful smile. Whatever Damian wanted to say to her would not take long; she would see to that.

When everyone had gone, she turned a seething glare in Damian's direction. "Whatever you have to say, you'd better make it quick. Harry's just itching to get his hands around your throat."

Damian stood, tucking his hands into his pockets. "Ah yes . . . Harry. As good a place to start as any."

"If you think I'm going to stand here and justify myself to you, think again."

"Our whole relationship was a big lie, wasn't it? Married to Harry." He made a sound of disgust, "I should have known he was your brother—hell, the two of you look enough alike."

"And what about you, Mr. Lynch, I guess you were completely truthful from the start."

"At least I had a good reason for not telling you who I really was," he snarled. "I wanted you to see me, not the celebrity."

Alana walked across the room. She needed to put some distance between them. She still hadn't fully accepted that her hero, Lynch, was this disturbing man, the one she wanted, needed . . . loved.

"Look," she said, turning to face him, "this has all been a terrible mistake. Let's not turn it into a national disaster. Our relationship was a fantasy; this is the real world, now. This is what I have to live with every day." She swept her hands out in a wild gesture, "Rules, ethics, propriety, things you have no understanding of." She paused for a minute when he made no response. "We had a good time together. Let's not spoil our memories by forcing a marriage that neither of us wants."

His face hardened. "You should have thought of that before you slapped me in front of millions of people."

"There could only have been two hundred people in that room," Alana said, shooting him a withering glance.

"There were international film crews there, as you well know."

Alana gasped. She had forgotten.

"Exactly," he said mockingly. "So you see, neither of us has a choice now. My publicity people can doctor what happened on the stage, but only if we end up tying the knot. So, like it or not, Miss Britton, we're going to get married." His voice was hard and determined. "I told you once that my work came before everything else, and I meant it. I won't let anything jeopardize my career, not even a delicious little slip of a girl like you."

"I'll apologize on TV, but I will not marry you." She would not marry a man who was participating in the event just so his professional image should remain unblemished.

"You will."

There was an expression on his face that she didn't like, but her temper was beginning to simmer, so she became even more defiant. "And how do you propose to make me? The days of beating women into submission are long gone. Besides . . ."—and she became a little cocky—"one word from me, and Harry would gladly flatten you." She would never let her brother hurt him, but he was not to know that.

"You and your dear brother seem to be attached at the hip," Damian said with derisive candor.

"You're disgusting," Alana spat. "You wouldn't recognize a clean, honest emotion if it raised up and bit you on the leg."

"I guess that's why you ran off and left me without a word in Berbice," he rasped, "because you're so full of good, honest emotions."

"I'm not going to discuss this with you any longer." Alana was almost in tears, and she was loath to let him see that his cruel words had any effect at all. "There will be no marriage between us, and that's my final word."

"We'll see." His voice crackled with menace; it was as though he had just accepted the gauntlet which she had so recklessly tossed at his feet.

Fourteen

Dinner was a tense affair, and Alana was certain that no one really noticed how delectable the meal was. The chef had outdone himself, but the food was like sawdust in her mouth. Harry sat beside her like a dark and beautiful avenging angel, and his strong presence was enough to put a definite damper on conversation. Damian himself was strangely quiet, and so was she, except for the occasional "pass the butter" comment. Her parents were the only ones who tried to inject an air of normalcy into the rather frigid proceedings. Nothing more was said of marriage, and, by the end of the evening, Alana felt secure in the knowledge that she'd won.

The next day, she received the shock of her life. She'd had a restless night, and had wandered downstairs early to take a quick peek at the newspaper before the rest of the household did.

Staring right at her from the front pages of the national newspaper in large bold print, was the declaration: "Alana Britton to wed author D.C. Lynch." She didn't pause to look at the photograph that had been printed underneath the statement; her eyes jumped right to the article, and her anger skyrocketed as she read. The passage ended with: "the happy couple do not have plans for a long engagement; a May wedding has been scheduled. They will reside in the United States."

For a long while, she stood frozen by disbelief. How foolish she had been to think that Damian would simply give up and accept the fact that she had no desire to be married to him. She should have known that he was capable of this kind of underhanded, despicable behavior. He was setting himself up as a victim in the press so that she would have no alternative but to go along with his absurd demands. And live in the United States? Was he completely crazy? Even if she was in agreement with this marriage, she couldn't live there. Guyana needed her professional skills; besides, she couldn't bear the thought of living somewhere else permanently. She had to think of some way of reasoning with Damian. His pride had been hurt, so this was his way of retaliating. But maybe, if she tried, she might be able to talk some sense into him. The night's passage had helped her to look at things very logically, and she was horrified by the terrible mess that she had made of things. Slapping D.C. Lynch on stage—Lord, what could she have been thinking? Even though Lynch was Damian, and she accepted that now, she should never have given in to her anger.

In half an hour, she was bathed and dressed. It was still quite early and, after the confusing events of the previous night, Alana was distinctly grateful that no one had risen yet. A few minutes later, she stood on the stairs outside Damian's little cottage in Llamaha Gardens. This time Peters came to the door with her, and waited until there was an answer. The door swung back and Damian stood there, half dressed but seemingly quite wide awake. He didn't appear at all surprised to see her, but his glance flickered over Peters, and his lips tightened.

"Your bodyguard, I guess?"

"Yes, sir," Peters said, his face breaking into a wide smile. "And can I say that it's indeed a great pleasure to finally meet you. I've read most of your books."

Damian nodded at Peters, then stepped back to allow Alana to enter.

"Is he the one who's been following us all these months?"

Alana gave him a startled look. "You knew?"

"I knew. At the time, I was debating whether or not to let you know that your 'husband' was having you followed . . . fool that I was."

Alana sighed. His mood hadn't improved a bit; this was going to be decidedly more difficult than she had originally imagined.

"Have you seen the newspaper this morning?" she asked, taking a seat. He didn't reply until he had seated himself at the little desk beneath the window. The morning sun streamed brightly into the room, and it was only then that she noticed that he had dark shadows beneath his eyes.

"I've seen it."

So he was going to be difficult. Alana knew that she really should be angry, but the bleak expression on his face left her feeling nothing but deep concern, and regret that she had caused him any pain.

"Did you sleep last night?"

She decided to change tactics. He wasn't, after all, completely immune to her. He might not love her, might even despise her, but she was certain that she still had the ability to attract him.

"I wrote all night."

This was what she had dreamed of since she'd read

the first Lynch novel—to be able to sit and discuss his ideas with him—and yet here she was now with the author himself, and she found that she had no desire to do anything but try to erase the harsh expression from his face.

She stood suddenly. "I'll make you something to eat."

He gave her a sharp look. "Why? You wouldn't harm your favorite author, would you?"

"What?" Alana had no idea what he was rambling about now.

"Well," he drawled, "it would be a very convenient way of getting me off your back. No Damian, no marriage."

Alana ground her teeth. "If I thought you were serious, I'd . . . I'd. . . ."

"Slap me again?" he asked, with a mocking twist of his lips.

"Don't forget that got us into this mess in the first place."

"And we could easily get out of it, if you weren't so damn stubborn."

He twisted in the chair and, for a minute, a flash of pain crossed his face. "Come over here and rub my back; it hurts." His eyes glinted at her in a grim, yet persuasive, manner.

"Get Stacy to rub it." She didn't want to touch him. Strange things happened to her when she was in his arms. She had to keep her wits about her, had to convince him to give up this ridiculous notion of marriage.

"Stacy's my agent. Besides, you're the one I want."

"Damian we have to talk about this."

"We'll talk . . . afterward."

He was the most difficult man to figure out. She wasn't sure whether he was still angry, and was just playing a perverse game of cat and mouse with her, or if he had finally realized the stupidity of their situation.

She placed her hands on the back of his neck and massaged, her hands moving in slow, soothing circles. He relaxed against her, and closed his eyes.

"Damian?"

"Uhmm?" He sounded half asleep.

"About this wedding . . ."

"What kind do you want?" he mumbled huskily.

Alana's hands stilled, and he uttered a sound of encouragement, and her hands went back to their rhythm.

"Damian, you're not listening to me."

"I am."

Alana shook him slightly, and he opened his eyes.

"Damian, we can't get married, surely you must understand that?"

He spun in the chair without warning, trapping her between his long legs.

"Why not?"

Alana's pulse rate skyrocketed as she stared into his deep black eyes and felt the throb of his heart beneath her fingers.

"We don't love each other. I want to love the man I marry."

"Love." He sounded suddenly bitter. "Why is that so important? We have other things going for us."

"Physical attraction isn't enough. Sex isn't enough," she said tremulously.

"And love is?"

"Yes."

"And you don't feel that for me?"

Alana swallowed, willing the lie to emerge without so much as a tremor.

"No. And you don't feel that for me, either."

He was silent for a long moment, his face becoming shuttered and hard; then he spoke with sudden conviction. "We'll have to do without it, then."

Alana scoured her brain, searching for something else to fight him with, to shake him back to reality.

"You told me yourself that you'd never get married."

"I've changed my mind," he said, with a silky note to his voice. "It's not only a woman's prerogative, you know."

"You don't just change your mind about something as fundamental as marriage," she snapped back at him.

"I do."

She was becoming desperate, and struck out wildly, seizing on anything. "I won't live in the United States. I can't; Guyana needs me . . . Harry needs me."

He released her suddenly, and stood towering over her.

"Harry, Harry, Harry! It's always Harry, isn't it? Everything comes back to him."

"He's my brother, and I love him."

"And there's only room enough for one man in that heart of yours?" He shoved his hands into his pockets and went to stare moodily out the window.

If she didn't know better, Alana would have sworn that he was jealous of her relationship with her brother. But that, of course, made no sense. That would mean that his feelings for her ran deeper than she thought . . . but, of course, they didn't. This was just typical Damian, possessive and selfish.

He turned from his perusal of the garden after a few minutes of silence. "We'll live here, then," he said abruptly, "or wherever you damn well choose."

"Don't swear at me," Alana responded, her patience almost exhausted. "And we're not living here or anywhere else, because I'm not going to marry you."

He came to stand directly before her, and they stood for wordless seconds, glaring at each other. Then, surprisingly, he laughed, a deep hearty sound which broke the silence of the morning.

"Mrs. Curten was right, you are a stubborn little cuss. We're going to enjoy being married."

Mrs. Curten. Everything made sense to Alana now. That was how he had known who she was. But, before she could question him on that, he had gathered her into his arms, and his lips were on hers, claiming them in a burningly sweet caress that she tried her best to resist but found herself returning, nevertheless. After mindless seconds, he raised his head, and his eyes were serious.

"Love can grow, Alana. Why don't you give it a chance? You might even find that, one day, you come to care for me almost as much as you do Harry."

Was he no longer thinking of their future relationship simply as a practical solution? Could he actually grow to love her, or was this simply a ploy to get her to give in to his demands? She wanted to believe that he could, but she didn't trust him. Life would be simply miserable, tied to a man who felt trapped by her presence, and who maybe ran around having paltry affairs with every other woman.

"I don't want to be chewing gum on your shoe." He had used that very expression once when she had questioned him on his feelings toward virgins.

"What?" His eyes were puzzled, and she could see that he didn't remember saying it. He pulled her closer, and she was enveloped in the heat of his body. She was weak, because she wanted this, and she didn't pull away as she knew she probably should. He bent and kissed the side of her mouth, and she was hard-pressed not to turn and meet his descending lips with her own.

"Marry me?"

"You don't get along with Harry," she demurred, and her resolve slipped a fraction.

"That particular young man has taken a distinct dislike to me, but I'll try for your sake."

"You're very alike."

"Me and Harry?" He seemed almost shocked by the suggestion.

Alana nodded. "That's why it's strange that you two don't get along."

"Nothing strange about that. We don't get along because of you."

She shook her head to clear the fog that was beginning to descend around her. She had to be strong. He was getting to her. His husky voice, intimate manner, hard, muscled body. She was on the verge of throwing caution to the wind.

"I'd lied to you," she said with something like desperation in her voice.

"And I didn't tell you the whole truth about who I was, so we're even."

There had to be something else. Some other thing she could throw at him to hold him at bay. "You said you were leaving, remember? That our relationship was wrecking your work."

She could see the determination on his face; he had decided to marry her, no matter what objections she threw his way.

"Do you remember every single thing I ever said?"

He was going to kiss her again. And he was doing it deliberately, with a studied calculation, because he knew that, when their lips were together, he was in complete control. She had to stop him. There had to be some way to get through to him. She didn't want to be miserable for the rest of her life, she wanted love and friendship, and passion and . . . and a meeting of the minds. Things that most other people wanted, too. And she wouldn't have these with Damian, couldn't have them with him, because he was a cynic, a man who had no time or inclination for love. God only knew what he thought marriage to her would be like. Maybe some sort of wild spiral between his writing and their bed, with a few meals thrown in here and there. And children. She hadn't thought about that before. Did he want them?

"No." She didn't realize she had spoken aloud. He was looking at her with a strange expression in his eyes.

"No, what?"

"I can't. We couldn't." She knew she wasn't making any sense, and she hastened to add, "You'd have affairs. I couldn't stand that."

He subjected her to a punishing smile. "Why would I need another woman, with you around?"

"Don't ask me; you're the one who should know."

"I don't need another woman." He paused and looked deep into her eyes, stirring her heart to a frenetic pounding. "I don't want any other woman but you."

Alana looked away from the compelling depths of his eyes. Oh, he was a sly one, all right. He knew exactly what to say to her, and she wanted so badly to believe him.

"It wouldn't work. We'd come to hate each other, and I couldn't bear that."

"My capacity for hatred, when it comes to you, is minimal, and I would give you no reason to hate me."

"Okay."

She hadn't really said that, surely? She must be crazy. She couldn't marry him.

But he'd heard her, and it was too late to say she hadn't meant it. She did mean it, but only deep inside, to herself, never aloud for him to hear. He grasped her about the waist, and swung her around.

"I knew you'd see the sense of this, eventually. Love isn't all-important."

Fifteen

From then on, things swept ahead in a whirlwind of arrangements, fittings, parties, and more arrangements. Her mother took charge, handling everything. Alana hardly saw Damian alone for two minutes at a time, and Harry kept his distance from the entire proceedings. They were to be wed at the Brickdam Cathedral in the middle of town. It was going to be a lavish affair, with guests flying in from around the world. Ambassadors and the like, and even an Arabian sheik who had befriended Alana when she was a small child. Damian's list of invitees included several literary greats who couldn't quite believe that he was actually getting married and had to be there to see the event for themselves, and, of course, his sister, who would arrive from Pennsylvania on the night before the wedding.

The speed with which everything had spiraled from a small, quiet ceremony with a few friends to a huge media event, which could possibly rival several "royal" weddings, was frightening. Alana had tried to get Damian alone on several occasions to discuss things with him, but it was virtually impossible. She had been told that protocol forbade that Damian see her before

the wedding and, save sneaking over to his cottage in
the dead of night, there was little that she could do.

She had managed to speak to him a few times on the
phone, but had been unable to gauge his receptiveness
to the gala event that their wedding had become. Somewhere in the back of her head, she had been hoping
that he would suddenly break into laughter and tell her
that it was all a big joke. They weren't really getting
married, after all. But he seemed to touch on every
other subject but that. How was she holding up under
the strain of things? Was she eating, and getting enough
rest? He even asked about Harry, something which surprised Alana a great deal. But never once did he even
intimate that he regretted their impending marriage,
and was willing to call it off.

So, when the day of the wedding actually arrived,
Alana was in a high state of nerves. First of all, the day
started out badly. Harry had come to her suite while
she was still asleep, and had begged, then insisted that
she not go through with marriage to Damian. He ran
down a long list of problems which he said she was
bound to encounter, married to a literary playboy who
felt no love for her. By the time he had left, Alana was
close to tears, because she knew that everything her
brother had said was true. She had thought those exact
things herself—she had even mentioned a few of them
to Damian—but he had swept them all away with a
laugh, while looking at her in the burningly intense way
that he usually did.

It was a terrifying thought that, in less than two hours,
she, Alana Britton, would be walking down the aisle,
clothed in white silk and beaded lace, and that at the

end of that long walk would be a man who had told her on many occasions that he didn't believe in love, in fact, had no time for it. How could marriage to him last without that essential ingredient? She had met his sister just the night before, and she had seemed so warm and pleasant. She had welcomed Alana into the family, then had congratulated her on being the one to steal her errant brother's heart. Alana had been acutely embarrassed, and hadn't the heart to tell the sweet woman that she had not in fact done that.

Knowing that her parents, and just about everyone besides Harry, thought that she and Damian were wildly in love contributed to the spurt of panic Alana felt as she heard the first strains of the organ as she stood in the anteroom of the cathedral. Her mother secured the flowing white veil atop her head, slipped the blue elastic garter belt which she had worn at her own wedding onto Alana's thigh, then stood back with tears in her eyes as the doors swept open, and Alana was confronted by what seemed like miles of pews with thousands of people all seated, waiting. Her father appeared at her side, big and solid, and he gave her hand a squeeze. Alana wondered if he suspected that she was on the verge of bolting from the church. She looked around frantically for Harry, but then the organ struck again and there was no more time. The wedding march had begun. All eyes turned in her direction, including Damian's. He looked devilishly handsome in a black tuxedo with a starched white cravat and black satin cummerbund. His eyes seemed to find hers from all that distance away, and his were silently encouraging. She didn't stumble once, the entire way, and it was only when she stood next to him, and he turned to her with a smile in his eyes and took her hand in his, that she felt her legs wobble dangerously. She was trembling

and, to her enormous surprise, so was he. He squeezed
her hand, as her father had done. Then the pastor was
asking them to repeat their vows. The clergyman asked,
"Who gives this woman?" and her father said that he
did. Then the pastor said, "If there be anyone here
who knows why this couple should not be wed, speak
now, or forever hold his peace," and Alana almost sank
into the floor when she heard her brother's voice.

There was an immediate ripple of sound as Harry
approached the altar. And Alana could see, from the
corner of her eye, that several people were attempting
to block his path, in as discreet a manner as was possible. Damian dropped her hand, and was away from her
before she could caution him with a single word. Alana
prayed that there wouldn't be a brawl in the church.
Surely Harry wouldn't. Alana closed her eyes, and only
opened them when she felt a touch on her arm. It was
the pastor.

"Don't worry, dear," he said in that warm, kind voice
which Alana knew so well, "they've gone into my office
behind the pulpit. Really, I've never seen anyone handle
your brother quite so effectively before. It was quite
marvelous to watch."

A few minutes later, Damian emerged unruffled, followed by a distinctly subdued-looking Harry. Alana shot
him a lightning glance. What had gone on in that
room? She had been certain that Damian's clothes
would've been in tatters, and that half the furniture in
the place would have required replacement. But there
was nary a seam out of place on him.

Damian grinned apologetically at the gathering, then
asked Father MacIntyre to continue. The remainder of
the proceedings went by without a hitch. It was a double
ring ceremony, unusual for Guyana. Alana placed the

solid band of gold on one of Damian's strong fingers, and he reciprocated with a smaller version of his own. Then he read a piece of verse which he'd written especially for her, and Alana felt ridiculous tears pool in her eyes as he poetically pledged to spend the rest of his life with her. It was the best piece of Lynch she'd ever heard, and the tragedy about it was that only she knew that it was completely insincere.

Afterward, they went on to the reception which was being held at the President's mansion. There were photographs of Alana and Damian, more shots of the entire family together with Alana sandwiched between Damian and Harry, then still more shots of the cutting of the six-tier traditional Guyanese wedding cake, a beautifully ivory-iced black cake, so called because its montage of rums and local fruits gave it a thick delicious texture and a deep, dark color.

Alana managed to weather the throng of well-wishers, and to keep her smile firmly in place. To everyone she was a radiant bride with an adoring husband who couldn't bear to let her out of his sight for even a few minutes. She tried to catch her brother's eye on several occasions, but gave up when it seemed clear that he was avoiding her. Whatever had occurred in that room between Damian and himself, he certainly was not in a hurry to divulge it to her.

Finally, with all the other proprieties observed, it was time for the dancing to begin, and everyone lined the floor of the giant ballroom and waited for the bride and groom to lead off. Damian swept Alana into his arms, and the lights were dimmed. She lifted the long train of her dress across one arm, and everyone cheered

loudly as Damian bent and captured her lips in a prolonged kiss. When he lifted his head, Alana was flustered and a bit embarrassed. Damian cocked a quizzical
eyebrow at her. "We're allowed to do that in public now,
you know. We're husband and wife. All perfectly legal
and moral," he added as an afterthought.

Alana felt a slight shudder run through her at his
words, his arms tightened around her in response.

"Cold?" he questioned.

She shook her head, and tried not to think about the
fact that she was actually married to this man. It wasn't
real to her yet. Maybe she would awaken soon, and find
that it had all been a dream, a peculiar, bittersweet farce.

"You look about as happy as a condemned prisoner
at his own hanging," Damian said after awhile. "Alana,
life with me won't be as bad as you think." He paused
and tipped her chin up so that he could examine the
glittering depths of her eyes. "In time, you might even
come to love me." There was a note of fragile hope in
his voice, and Alana felt like screaming at him. How
could he even imagine that she would have agreed to
this marriage if she didn't already love him?

Later, he pulled her away from the crowd and said,
with a hint of mischief in his voice, "Time to leave."

Alana gave him a startled look. "So soon?" It wasn't
yet six P.M.

"We'll miss our flight if we don't."

"Flight?" she asked, not quite understanding what
he was saying.

"Our honeymoon in Trinidad and Tobago."

Alana's heart leapt, despite herself. This time they
would be able to do their exploring in a leisurely manner. They would get Phil again, of course. Maybe he'd
be able to show them the entire island this time. To-

bago, too, and all the other nooks and crannies which they hadn't had the time to see the first time.

"Why didn't you tell me before? I haven't packed or anything."

"It was supposed to be a surprise. Your clothes are already at the beach chateau in Tobago." He saw the question in her eyes, and answered it before she had a chance to ask. "And Phil, the very industrious taxi driver, is already there, just waiting to pick us up from the airport."

Alana smiled. "Well, he is the best damn taxi driver in all of Trinidad and Tobago."

Damian nodded in agreement, his face as serious as Phil's often was whenever he was especially earnest about making his point. "The best damn taxi driver."

There was a polite cough, and they both turned in unison. Alana struggled to keep a straight face. Harry was obviously wondering why it was that they were standing so close together, quietly exchanging swear words.

"I'll explain it to you later," she mouthed at him.

Harry's eyebrows rose marginally, but he extended a hand to Damian.

"Good luck to you, brother-in-law."

Damian shook his hand heartily, and Alana's eyes glistened with sudden unshed tears. They might learn to be friends after all.

"I'll take extra special care of Alana," Damian was saying, and he clapped Harry on the shoulder to emphasize the seriousness of his intention.

Harry nodded, then held out his arms to Alana. She sped into them without further encouragement. Harry hugged her for a long moment, then kissed her soundly on the cheek.

"He's not as bad as all that," he whispered, "but let me know if he doesn't make you happy."

They held each other for a few more seconds, then Harry whispered, "You'd better go."

It took Alana a few minutes to change into her travel clothes. They both said a quick goodbye to her parents, then they were off to the airport, and aboard a luxury liner in next to no time. The entire first-class cabin was empty, and Damian seated her by a spacious window seat, then said with a lazy smile, "We've come full circle, I think."

Alana kicked off her shoes and flexed her toes.

"Yes, and I remember thinking then what a complete fool I'd made of myself in that duty-free shop."

Damian grinned. "If it hadn't been for that, you probably wouldn't have spoken to me at all on the plane, and all my trouble would have been for nothing."

Alana stared at him. "You mean you . . ."

Damian nodded. "I wasn't supposed to be on your flight at all. My flight into Trinidad and Tobago was scheduled to leave half an hour after yours. I got them to switch me. Luckily your flight was almost half empty."

Alana blinked at him for a minute. Her heart was battering like a wild thing against her ribs.

"It wasn't chance at all, then, that we met?"

Damian picked up her hand and stroked his thumb lightly across her fingers. The band of gold on her left hand winked and glistened in the light of the cabin.

"I followed you into the shop. You were so entranced by the shelf of chocolates that you didn't even see me."

"But . . . I would have noticed you out in the terminal. I saw you right away in the shop."

"That was my intention. You stared at me with those huge, soft eyes, and my heart stopped beating for a second. For the next few minutes, my entire body was numb. When you stepped on my foot, I barely felt it."

Alana laughed. "I felt sure I'd broken your instep."

Damian nodded sagely. "I felt sure you had too, but only several hours later."

"You were wearing that pinstriped suit with the maroon tie."

"And I remember that you were wearing a white wooly dress, and one droplet of water trickling down right . . . there." He leaned across and traced the side of her face with his lips. And Alana felt her mouth curve involuntarily into a smile.

"You are a very hard man not to . . . like." She had almost given herself away, and said "love."

Damian pulled her into his arms so that her head rested on his chest. His eyes glittered down at her. "And I'm an even easier one to love." He paused to pull the pins from her hair, then he threaded his fingers through until they rested against her scalp. "Say you'll always stay with me Lani . . . even if . . ."—he paused, as though he were feeling for the right words. "I know the first time we made love, I scared you. I wanted you so much that I must have hurt you. I was going to ask you to marry me in Berbice, but you ran away, and I panicked. I thought I'd lost you." He stopped as though he was unsure of how to go on.

Alana stroked his face. She still couldn't believe what she was hearing. What he wasn't saying.

"But, I left because I thought that you didn't care," she said softly. "And when you said you had to return to Georgetown at the end of the week, I just assumed that you were telling me gently that it was all over between us. You had said that you were going to leave, remember?"

Damian gave a hoarse bark of laughter. "Leave? I was just fooling myself. My writing dwindled to nothing, because suddenly the future seemed bleak and empty without you. There was no pool of inspiration from which to draw."

"Why didn't you let me know who you were from the beginning?" It was a question that had been bothering her for some time.

"I wanted you to care about me for myself, and not because you were bowled over by the great 'Lynch.' Of course at the time, I had no idea who you were. I knew from the start that you weren't being totally honest with me, but I was so jealous of Harry that I couldn't think straight."

The plane started with a jolt, and Alana cuddled closer to him. "We've both been total idiots, haven't we?" She pressed a kiss to his neck, and a shudder went through him. "What did you say to Harry in Father McIntyre's office?" She had to know.

"Just something that I should have told you ages ago."

Alana looked at him expectantly.

"I told him that, from now on, he'd just have to get used to the idea of me being around, because I was going to stay around until I made you love me as much as I loved you."

Alana's eyes rounded, and her lips parted in a silent "O." "But I do love you, Damian, I have almost from the start."

It was his turn to look surprised. "Harry never said . . ."

But she didn't let him finish. "Harry never would. He knew that I'd want to be the one to tell you myself."

For a minute, there was doubt in Damian's eyes, and a flash of jealousy which Alana now recognized.

"Do you love me as much as Harry?"

Alana smiled and pulled his head down to hers. "At least as much," she said, then proceeded to demonstrate very thoroughly what she meant. A few minutes later she asked, with a cheeky grin, "Convinced?"

Damian pulled her close again, his eyes fastening on her lips. "Not yet."

A few hours later, Alana showed him again how much she did love him, and Damian reciprocated in kind. And in the shroud of night somewhere outside their bedroom window, the glittering blue ocean whispered, silent and mysterious, capturing and keeping forever secret the murmurs of love and the promises that would linger and keep them strong and together for a lifetime.

About the Author

Níqui Stanhope was born in Jamaica, West Indies, but grew up in a small bauxite mining town in Guyana, South America. Because her parents traveled quite a bit, and always took the entire family along, the summers of her childhood were spent exploring the rich culture of the Caribbean and South America. In 1984 she emigrated to the United States with her family. She admits that novel writing never occurred to her until after she had graduated from the University of Southern California with a degree in chemistry.

Níqui Stanhope now lives in Los Angeles. *Night to Remember* is her first book.

Look for these upcoming Arabesque titles:

February 1998

HEART OF THE FALCON by Francis Ray
A PRIVATE AFFAIR by Donna Hill
RENDEZVOUS by Bridget Anderson
I DO! A Valentine's Day Collection

March 1998

KEEPING SECRETS by Carmen Green
SILVER LOVE by Layle Giusto
PRIVATE LIES by Robyn Amos
SWEET SURRENDER by Angela Winters

April 1998

A PUBLIC AFFAIR by Margie Walker
OBSESSION by Gwynne Forster
CHERISH by Crystal Wilson Harris
REMEMBRANCE by Marcia King-Gamble